To a special daughter,
R...

Love, ...

A SUMMER GHOST

ff

A SUMMER GHOST

Ruth Tomalin

faber and faber
LONDON · BOSTON

First published in 1986
by Faber and Faber Limited
3 Queen Square London WC1N 3AU

Photoset by Parker Typesetting Service, Leicester
Printed in Great Britain by Mackays of Chatham
All rights reserved

British Library Cataloguing in Publication Data

Tomalin, Ruth
A summer ghost.
I. Title
823'.914[J]   PZ7
ISBN 0-571-13826-8

Library of Congress Cataloging-in-Publication Data

Tomalin, Ruth.
A summer ghost.
Summary: Reluctant to leave her beloved pony when her family goes on
vacation, Arabella manages to stay behind, without her parents'
knowledge, but comes to regret her stolen holiday when she begins to
suspect there is a ghost in the house.
[1. Ghosts—Fiction.   2. Horses—Fiction.   3. Country life—Fiction.
4. England—Fiction]   I. Title. PZ7.T583Su   1986   [Fic]
85-27430   ISBN 0-571-13826-8

The beeches know the accustomed head
Which loved them, and a peopled air
Beneath their benediction spread
Comforts the silence everywhere;
  For native ghosts return and these
  Perfect the mystery in the trees.

Hilaire Belloc

To Annabel and Miranda

Acknowledgements

The epigraph is taken from *The Four Men* by Hilaire Belloc
and is reprinted by permission of A. D. Peters & Co Ltd.
The Wandering Knight's Song, quoted on page 106, is by
J. G. Lockhart (1794–1854).

Contents

1

Morning in London

Arabella woke early because Berry was bouncing on her bed, singing –

> "Arab Ella, Arab Ella,
> Have you packed your sun umbrella?" –

and then –

> "Arab Ella, Arab Ella,
> Air-sick, sun-struck, greeny-yella –"

He paused to give her a chance to hit out. But Arabella only lay there sadly, with her eyes shut, thinking – In a few hours, we'll be on the plane. Flying off to France. It *is* going to happen after all. Nothing can stop it now.

A hollow feeling of misery crept through her.

Today should have been the best day of the year: the day they left London to spend six weeks at Timewells, their cottage in Sussex. They went there most week-ends as well; but the summer holidays were special.

Arabella looked forward all the year to those six weeks. Busy friendly mornings at the riding-school. Long afternoons climbing trees, or messing about in the stream with Berry. Moonlight picnics on the downs, or on the beach at Wittering. Wet days in the stable loft, reading Dad's old *William* books. The time always went far too quickly; and yet, in another way, it seemed to go on for ever.

And now, instead, she was getting – what?

A month at Sauterelle, in the south of France, in blazing dazzling heat, beside a glittering sea. A wasted month, on a boring crowded beach, or in the noisy sea-front playgrounds that Berry adored. Endless sunshine and cloudless skies: or, for her, the hot headachy shade of a beach umbrella.

It was all right for the others. Ned and Karen and Berry loved the heat. Like Dad, they were as dark as gypsies, with the kind of skin that never burns, but takes on a beautiful nut-brown tan, even on breezy Sussex beaches.

But Arabella, fair and pale, felt like a ghost among the sun-tanned summer crowds. She quite liked swimming; but not all day long, even if they'd let her. Besides, she hated that clear bright light. Most of the time she seemed to be just mooching around, longing for Timewells, for shady trees and streams, and especially for her old pony, Baggins.

Today it was all starting again; but much worse, because Mum wouldn't be there. She didn't care for too much sun either. Last summer, when they'd all spent a fortnight together at Sauterelle, she and Arabella had shared the beach umbrella. But now Dad and Mum had flown off to visit Uncle Hugh in New Zealand, and they wouldn't be back till the end of August.

She gave a little groan.

Berry, pleased at this sign of life, began another of those rhymes they'd made up to tease her, one day last summer. Berry never knew when a joke had had its day.

> "Sauterelle is hot as hell-a,
> Far too hot for Arab Ella . . ."

This time, she opened her eyes and said, "Stop it. Shut up. Or –"

He gave a challenging bounce. "Or what?"

She looked across at the luggage standing ready – her back-pack, Berry's airline bag – and shut her eyes again, too sad to answer.

Berry poked her with his foot. "Yes? Or what?"

"Or – I'll be postman. I'll take in all the letters. Every day. I warn you."

Berry went quiet at this threat.

He was the family postman. He'd started this game last December, in the heady weeks of the Christmas post; and he'd never grown tired of it. Every morning he picked up the letters at the front door, and doled them out.

He cried, "You won't. I shan't let you."

"Can't stop me. I'm twice your age."

He said in a small voice, "How long for?"

"Always. And I shan't let you post anything for me. Not ever."

After a sulky minute, he began to tap out *Arab Ella*, *Arab Ella* with his knuckles on the bedroom wall.

She followed up her success, saying briskly, "You can stop that, too."

"Or – what else?"

"Or you'll wake poor Ginette. *Again*."

They glared at each other, then began to laugh.

Ginette had come over to take them all to Sauterelle, to her parents' hotel. She was sleeping next door, in Arabella's room; Arabella had moved in with Berry. At midnight last night Ginette had roused the house with shrieks, because Bravey, the garden cat, had arrived on her bed with a live grasshopper.

So far as a cat can be anyone's, Bravey was Arabella's cat. He often climbed up to visit her at night, bringing a mouse or a moth or other prey for her to see. Her window was kept screwed open a few inches at the bottom, so that he could squeeze in.

Ginette had stayed with the family in other summers, as

13

au pair girl, to improve her English. This was now good enough for her to say exactly what she thought of Arabella, Bravey and the grasshopper. She did so with some bitterness: she'd never liked Arabella.

They had all helped to shoo the intruders back into the garden. Ned took out the screws and shut the window, and Karen said the right, polite things: she was good at that.

But it wasn't a happy start to the holiday. Now, Arabella soon stopped laughing. Weeks on that horrible beach, with Ginette in charge, cross with her already . . . Her parents were nice, but one wouldn't see much of them; they were so busy running their hotel.

One good thing: Bravey wouldn't really miss her. Neighbours would feed him and talk to him. She was the one who'd miss *him*.

It was the same with the pony, Baggins, who lived in a farmer's field at Timewells. She always hated leaving him. On Sunday evenings, there would be a heart-rending ten minutes known in the family as "Arab's Farewell to her Steed". In London, aching, she read books about how to pick out your pony's feet and get the mud off his coat.

Steps on the path below . . . the letter-box rattled. Berry dashed out of the room. On the landing, he lifted his voice again in a mocking chant –

> "Pale as porridge or paella,
> Like a mushroom in a cellar –

ow! ouch! ooooooh . . ."

His song changed to yelps, then wails. Arabella had sprung out of bed, caught him at the top of the stairs, pushed him aside and rushed down.

There was just one letter in the box. One thin blue air-mail envelope. Arabella swooped on it. She read on the back, *Sender, Lucy Buckley.* A letter from Mum, already! Posted in Christchurch, New Zealand, only five days ago. Then she saw the name on the envelope.

It wasn't addressed to Ginette, or Ned, or all of them together. It was for *her.* Arabella Buckley.

2

Air-letters

Months ago, when they'd been told of the holiday plans, Arabella had cried at once, "But why *me*? Why do I have to go there? You know I don't want to. Can't I just stay at Timewells?"

"No, no, Arab. Not all by yourself. You're not old enough."

"I needn't be by myself. Can't Mrs Hat sleep there too?"

When the Buckleys were away, a neighbour kept an eye on the cottage, going in each day to air the rooms and do a little dusting. If a letter came she would send it on, writing on the back of the envelope, "All well here. H. Atkins." The family called her Mrs Hatpins: Mrs Hat for short.

"Not this year," Mum told Arabella. "Eleven is *really* too young. Another time, perhaps."

But she went on arguing and grumbling, until Mum said:

"Oh dear. I didn't realize you hated it quite so much. Perhaps I'd better stay behind this time."

That made Ned and Karen furious. They got Arabella by herself and told her she *must* stop making a fuss.

"Don't you see? – you're going to ruin Mum's holiday. The first she's had away from us, since Ned was born! Fifteen years! How'd you like to be stuck with a pack of kids, every summer for fifteen years?"

Arabella was shocked. "But Mum likes being with us!"

"Of course she does, dimwit! But that doesn't mean she won't enjoy a break. And now you're all set to spoil everything, nagging away at her. So belt up, will you?" Karen said kindly.

"Oh, it's all right for you three! Berry just wants to go screeching round with a lot of little kids. Sauterelle or Bognor, it's all the same to him. And *you*," she told Karen, "all you want is to show off in your new beach gear, to a lot of frog girls and boys – "

Karen grinned, not at all put out.

"And Ned! We all know *he* can't wait to see – "

She stopped suddenly. Ned had gone white. His face had a frozen look, waiting for her to finish.

Ned was in love. No one could help knowing that. He'd spent the whole time, last summer, sitting with a ring of other admirers, gazing at a beautiful French girl, Chantal. Sixteen at least, with tawny hair and golden eyes. A girl like a lioness . . .

But she found she couldn't talk about Chantal. Not right out like that – it would be cruel. She rushed on – "We all know you're hooked on wind-surfing, you'll have a fine time. So why can't I do what I want?"

"Poor old Arab," Karen said. "She wants to stay home and parade about at gymkhanas, grabbing all the cups, on her smart show pony . . ." This gave them both the giggles. Baggins was not that kind of pony.

Karen added, "Now look. If you'll lay off, just this once, I swear I'll help. And so will Ned. We'll get them to let you stay, next year. Fair enough?"

"Oh, next year!" Arabella grumbled. Next year was so far off, it didn't count.

She saw that she'd have to give in, at the moment. But she'd never lost hope. As the summer term went by, she still waited for Dad and Mum to say, "We've been thinking it over. Perhaps you're not too young after all . . ."

They hadn't said it. And now it was far too late. This morning, the minute she woke up, she'd known that nothing could save her.

Nothing? Standing there, gazing at the air-letter, she began to tremble. All her wild hopes were back again. She rushed into the study, locked the door, and stood a moment longer, clasping the envelope, half afraid to open it.

Mum had written to *her*. Suppose it was to say – that she could go to Timewells, after all?

The letter came open easily. The flap wasn't properly stuck, it lifted at a touch. She got the paper out.

Mum had taken her little typewriter with her. The letter was typed, and she skimmed through it quickly.

"Arabella dear, We've written to you all at Sauterelle, but I hope this will come in time to catch you at home, before you leave." (*Oh!* she breathed, *It's true! I can stay!*)

"Dad and I want to say a special word. We know you're not as happy about this holiday as the others. But you won't spoil things for *them*, will you? It's so kind of Madame to have you, and of Ginette –" She couldn't go on. Tears blinded her. She crunched the paper up, and let it drop.

The disappointment was so bad, she felt she could hardly bear it. The letter was just a sort of telling-off, really. Oh, if only it had said – it *ought* to have said –

She drifted over to the desk, opened a drawer and found a packet of blue air-mail paper. She fingered the old type-writer, then sat down and slid a page on to the roller.

Arabella could type quite well. She'd taught herself, a long time ago, in an idle time after chicken-pox; starting with rows of cats on walls –

– then going on to stories. They'd looked rather queer at first ("ONxe UPoon A t1mE TheR werre ' 8 * + CaTz & thay Wer? nameeD " etc.) but she was well past that stage now. She began to type the letter Mum should have sent.

"Arabella dear, Dad and I know you hate going to Sauterelle. So we've decided on a different plan. You can stay at Timewells, after all. We have rung Mrs Hat and it's all fixed. She will come in to sleep at nights. Have a lovely time. Lots of love, Mum."

She took out the letter and read it through. Then she thought, Mum wouldn't just write to me, she'd tell Ginette as well. She put in another sheet.

"Dear Ginette, There has been a change of plan. Arabella will be going to Timewells because she likes it best there. She can travel with you as far as Gatwick, then go on in the train. Mrs Atkins will expect her on the bus. Yours sincerely, Lucy Buckley."

The envelope said, "Miss Arabella Buckley". Above this, she typed carefully, "Mlle Ginette Rosier, and ".

She folded both sheets, put them into the envelope and stuck it down, properly this time, with a dab of glue. She yawned, and then laughed, shakily: a *hollow laugh*, she thought. Things never happened the way you wanted them. Letters like this were really air-letters, flimsy as day-dreams or castles in the air . . .

All the same, she felt better now. Typing was always fun.

Something gleamed on the carpet. A pin. She bent to pick it up, and stuck it in her pyjama top. There was a rhyme she'd heard somewhere –

> See a pin and pick it up,
> All the day you'll have good luck.

What a hope! – today, of all days. She tried out another hollow laugh.

Still, the thought of good luck was cheering. So, by now, was the thought of breakfast. She unlocked the door and went to chop up a fish finger, as a goodbye treat for Bravey.

3

A time to speak

Bravey had lived in the London garden, and the next-door gardens, for several years. He'd appeared there suddenly, very thin and starved and timid, no one knew from where. At first all the other cats set out to drive him away; especially a sleek vain Siamese from two doors down. It would pounce and hunt him, when he tried to drink the saucers of milk put out for him by the Buckleys.

Then Arabella persuaded Mum to buy liver for him every day, to feed him up. After a month on this diet, with a lot of petting added, he was a different animal, well able to stand up for himself; and the other cats left him in peace. Even the Siamese stayed away.

Arabella named him Bravey, and he settled down to enjoy life. When the Buckleys were away, he was looked after by Miss Hall next door.

Karen and Arabella were upstairs, finishing their packing, when they heard Miss Hall at the back door; she had come to fetch his dishes. The bedroom window was open, and they could hear Ginette telling Miss Hall:

"The cat has not eaten this morning."

This was true. When Arabella gave him the fish finger he'd rubbed his head against her hand – Bravey had beautiful manners – but he hadn't touched his breakfast. Now he was dozing on the grass patch by the back door.

Ginette went on, speaking rather loudly –

"It is a very old animal. I think it will not live long. Perhaps you should take it to – to the doctor?"

Miss Hall laughed. "Oh, there's nothing much wrong with Bravey. Just the hot weather, you know. No need to waste money on the vet."

"Not for medicine. That would be waste, yes," Ginette said flatly. "But I think he should be given something – you understand? – so that he will not linger."

Miss Hall sounded puzzled, then shocked.

"You surely don't mean – have him *put to sleep*? But what ever for? I'm sure there's nothing wrong . . ."

"He is old and ill. He cannot eat. It would be kinder to do this while the children are away. One need say nothing to them. He should not be left to suffer."

The crisp little sentences seemed to tinkle out, as sharp as ice or broken glass.

"Goodness! I wouldn't dream of such a thing. Arabella would be heart-broken." Miss Hall sounded quite upset by now.

Karen and Arabella looked at each other aghast. Ginette was actually plotting to have Bravey murdered. Thank heaven, Miss Hall could be trusted to take no notice.

Of course Ginette knew that quite well. And she knew Arabella couldn't help overhearing. It was her revenge for the grasshopper.

They raced downstairs. Miss Hall was looking pink and indignant. Ginette said:

"I have told Miss Hall – I do not think this cat is healthy."

Arabella let Karen deal with it. Shivering with anger, she didn't trust herself to speak. And she thought – I can't bear her. And she can't bear me. And we've got to be together for weeks. I don't see how I *can* . . . not after this.

Berry came rushing in, waving a letter.

"Look, look what I've found! For you, Ginette – *and* you, Arab – you never opened it! And look, on the back, it says

22

– look, that's Mum's name – Lucy Buckley – "

The air-letter . . . She'd forgotten all about it. She must have left it lying on the desk. Better explain quickly.

But she couldn't say a word. She stood there dully, watching, while Ginette took the letter, looked at the envelope, reached for a knife and slit it open. She took out the two sheets, glanced at them, handed one to Arabella and began to read the other.

Arabella stared down at the blue paper in her hand. "Arabella dear, Dad and I know you hate going to Sauterelle . . ." She drew a deep breath, ready to say:

"Look, it's not true. I typed them myself. It's just a joke . . ."

Still she said nothing. It was so hard to begin – and Ginette wasn't going to think it funny.

Ginette glanced through the few lines, frowned at the typed words *Lucy Buckley*, and then read the letter aloud. Then she looked at the sheet in Arabella's hand. Arabella, dumb, handed it over, and Ginette read that out too. She seemed taken aback – but not annoyed.

"Glad to be rid of me," Arabella saw. A pity it wouldn't really happen. Karen gasped:

"Oh Arab! Oh, lucky old you – just what you wanted! I never thought they'd change their minds – did you?" She snatched both letters and read them eagerly. Ned came in, and she cried, "Ned, look here!" He looked over her shoulder.

In a moment, Ned or Karen would begin to suspect. They'd spot the different sort of typing on the envelope. Oh well . . . it was being quite funny, while it lasted.

Karen exclaimed, "Oh, but her ticket – it'll be wasted! And her room in the hotel!"

Ginette shrugged, and said coolly, "In July? No *problème*."

"No," Karen agreed. "There'll be bags of takers, all queuing up to get them – "

"You mean," Berry shrieked, "*Queues* of takers with their *bags* . . ."

"So!" Ginette went on, "you are all ready? Ned, Karen – the luggage – our taxi will be here in five minutes. But first I must ring Mrs Atkins, to make sure all is understood."

Running up for the baggage, Karen called, "Her number's on the pad by the phone!"

Arabella smiled to herself. No need to own up after all. Mrs Hat would soon make it clear that there was no such plan. A good take-in for beastly Ginette, and serve her right.

She glanced at Ned, ready to share the joke; but Ned was looking aloof and absent-minded. She guessed suddenly that he was thinking – *We're going there now. I'll see Chantal tomorrow* . . . He followed Karen upstairs. Miss Hall was gone. Arabella stood in the doorway, waiting to hear that phone call. In a moment, Mrs Hat would be on the line, saying firmly, *I don't know what you're on about, Madamazelle*.

But it didn't happen.

Far away in Mrs Hat's cottage the phone rang and rang, and no one answered. Ginette dialled the Timewells number – Mrs Hat might be over there on her daily visit. But again there was no reply.

The taxi drew up; and then everything was happening at once. Ginette put down the phone and began to give orders. Everyone milled about with cases and hold-alls. Arabella slipped her pack on, and settled the straps.

They were in the taxi – Karen and Berry chattering excitedly – spinning past the Albert Hall, round Hyde Park Corner, down to Victoria . . . Ginette was getting tickets . . . they were queuing for the train . . . and then *in* the train, outside Victoria, bound for Gatwick Airport.

Now I've *got* to tell, Arabella realized. It's gone far enough, no one's going to think it funny now, only Berry perhaps. No, I'll wait till Gatwick, then Ginette will be so busy, she won't have time to be cross. I don't care, anyway.

Ginette suddenly looked at her and asked coldly:

"Did you take your pills?"

Her pills . . . she'd forgotten. If she took them now, quickly, she wouldn't feel sick in the plane. She fished in her pocket for the little package. But Karen interrupted —

"She doesn't need those, not for the train!"

Not for the train . . . She took her hand out of her pocket.

Suddenly it all seemed real. *They* thought she wouldn't be going in the plane. They thought she was going on to Timewells. It could be true, almost. She sat in a dream, gazing at nothing, like Ned.

Berry was kneeling at the window, looking out for a little white railway sign that said Stoat's Nest Junction. Soon after Purley, it was; he and Arabella pretended it belonged to a mini-railway, run by mice. Stoat's Nest was the danger spot on their journey. Here it came . . .

He turned to grin at her; but she didn't see. She wasn't taking any notice – not of him, nor the sign, nor anything. She seemed in a sort of daze.

The train rocked; Berry almost fell off the seat. He sat back, staring at her, and began acting up, to make her look at him. Arabella came out of her dream at last, and saw him making wild faces, waggling his hands and miming at her:

> "Good old funny Arabella,
>   *She's* not coming to Sauterelle-a."

4

Keeping quiet

"Gatwick!" someone exclaimed.

No, it couldn't be. Not so soon. Arabella jumped up in panic. She *must* explain: if only she'd done it straight away! It seemed pretty feeble now.

Everyone was ready to get out. She hitched the pack on her shoulders, and edged up to Ginette.

Ginette said, "No, Arabella. You will remain on this train. Here is your ticket. Now, pay attention – you must change at – "

"She knows!" Karen broke in. "We often come by train . . ."

"But – " Arabella stammered, "I'm not – I mean – "

Ginette held out the ticket, and gave her a look of pure dislike.

Arabella took the ticket. She dropped her pack, and sat down slowly. They were *getting out* . . . going without her . . . Karen winked at her, Berry aimed a friendly kick, even Ned came out of his trance to say, "Good luck, Arab."

All the day you'll have good luck . . .

Now they were all on the platform, lined up, waiting to wave her off – but Ginette wouldn't let them. She was rounding them up, heading them for the exit. A last shout from Berry – "Write to me" – and they were gone. She was alone.

The train throbbed and hummed, getting ready to start

again. Still time to jump out and rush after them.

No. Too late now. The train started.

A plane came roaring overhead. It couldn't be theirs, yet; but, she realized – I'm not flying, after all. Not going to France. I'm in Sussex, going to Timewells. "The further off from Gatwick, the nearer is to – *there*."

The carriage was almost empty now. The countryside flashed past. Yellow cornfields. Blue and pink flowers on the banks. Deer on the skyline . . . They stopped at a station, then another and another. At the eighth stop a lady got in and sat in the far corner. Arabella saw this was Pulborough. One more stop. Change for Chichester. Then the bus.

She realized that the new arrival was glancing across at her. Arabella turned to look out of the window. She couldn't bear to talk to anyone; not yet, anyway. She wanted to sit quietly and try to take in what had happened.

But the lady spoke.

"You're Lucy Buckley's little girl, aren't you?"

Arabella was too surprised to answer. She looked back at the smiling face. The lady moved, and came to sit down opposite. She beamed, "Karen, isn't it? What luck. I thought you were all away. You're the very person I need!"

The very person – how could she be? So far as she knew, she'd never seen this lady before. At least – she looked like a lot of others at Timber: bright blue eyes, short fair hair, navy trousers . . .

"You don't know me, I see," she smiled. "But I've seen you often in the village. Your mother and I help run the Autumn Fair, you know. Now!" She snapped her handbag open, rummaged and brought out a notebook and pencil – "Now, I want you to be very kind, and give me her address in New Zealand."

27

Mum's address? That was easy. Of course she'd learnt it off by heart: they all had. Tomorrow they'd be sending off postcards.

She was just going to recite it when . . . something made her hesitate. An alarm bell seemed to ring in her mind. For the moment she couldn't see why.

The lady didn't notice. She was chattering on, "You see – I've a sister in Christchurch. She'd simply love to meet your mother. I'll get in touch with her at once, and then she'll write to Mother. If you'll just tell me the address? And," she added, "of course, I'll write to Mother too, and tell her I've met you, and – "

Arabella didn't hear any more. It flashed on her – she mustn't, she *must not* let any such letter go off to New Zealand. Especially from a chatty person like this. She'd be bound to say something like – "I got in the train at Pulborough, and there was your little girl, all by herself . . ."

And then there would be real trouble. Phone calls to Sauterelle, all the way from Christchurch, costing pounds and pounds. It would all come out about those letters. Dad and Mum would think she'd plotted the whole thing, that she'd written them on purpose. What a row there'd be . . .

Much worse, though – Mum would be so worried, she might even fly straight home to Timewells. Her holiday would be ruined, after all. It would be *her* fault – and Ned and Karen would never let her forget it.

It simply mustn't happen.

The train was slowing for another station. Arundel. Arabella sprang to her feet, grabbing her pack with one hand and the door-catch with the other. She gasped,

"Look, I'm sorry – you've made a mistake – I'm not Karen anyone – I have to get out here, goodbye – "

She jumped, staggered, picked herself up and ran: down a long platform, over a bridge, past the barrier, out and away.

She found herself running along the edge of a busy road, towards a distant town and a castle on a hill. Cars whizzed by, trucks roared and rumbled; and her thoughts whirled.

She told herself in sheer horror – *Look what you've done!* And then: What's going to happen now?

She must get away somewhere quiet, and think things out. This wasn't a game any more, or a joke. What she'd done was serious, and now it was far too late to turn back.

5

Outlaw

Soon she reached a place where the road forked east and west. If she turned west, and kept on walking, she'd come to Timewells. Ten miles, about: could she walk as far as that?

Well, she must. But not in broad daylight, with cars passing all the time. Sooner or later, someone in one of the cars would know her. The nearer she got to home, the riskier it would be. And one thing was certain: she didn't want anyone else asking, "Aren't you Lucy Buckley's daughter?"

I'll wait till dark, she thought. It'll be safe then.

But this was July, and dark, or even dusk, would be a long time coming. She had to hide somewhere for hours and hours.

As she stood there, she heard an odd sound overhead, coming nearer. A soft, hoarse, pulsing sound, like – yes, like swans' wings. And that was what it was. Wild swans, three of them, dazzling white in the sun, flying so low that she could see their bright eyes and the separate feathers of their plumage. As she watched, one feather floated down, like a thistledown plume, and she caught it in her fingers.

The swans were out of sight now, behind a grove of trees. She followed through the dark leafy tunnel. Here the road ran under a steep wooded cliff, crowned by the turrets of a castle; on the other side there were reed-beds and glimpses of water. The air was filled with soft bird voices.

She couldn't see any birds; but, just ahead, there was a path leading away from the road, past a sign that said Wildfowl Reserve.

Now she was in a green sunlit marsh, with winding pathways, rushy hollows, mossy banks, low damp meadows and little woods. The birds were everywhere – swans, cygnets, geese, ducks, coots, moorhens with tiny fluffy black chicks; and they were all *wild*, yet calm and unafraid.

She came to a little hut, and went in. It was dark inside; and the far wall was all of glass, looking out on to a sparkling lake full of diving, swimming birds. She was in a *hide*: the very thing she needed. The birds couldn't see her – and nor could anyone else. She could stay here all day.

Gazing through the glass wall, safe as a moorhen in a reed-bed, the bird voices babbling in a gentle chorus, she thought – If only the others were here!

And then she seemed to wake with a jump. The others ... they'd be in the plane now. Or perhaps – how long had she been here? – they'd have landed, and now they were in a car, speeding towards Sauterelle. They were all right: but she was here alone, and all wrong.

Somewhere she'd heard a story about an outlaw, hiding in the reeds. That was what she was: an outlaw. She'd broken every kind of family rule. She must have been mad to let it happen...

How could she get back on the right side of the law? Go back to Gatwick, and get on the next plane for France? But she had no ticket now; and her passport was still in the travel file in Ginette's bag. She only had her holiday money – not nearly enough – and the ticket to Chichester: she hadn't given that up.

Perhaps – perhaps she really ought to go back to

London, and borrow her fare from Miss Hall? But there was still the missing passport. Miss Hall would be ringing Ginette in no time. At the thought of all the fuss, her heart sank.

Well, there was one other thing she could do. She could go on home to Timewells, and just stay there quietly, out of sight, till the family came home. That was what she wanted most in the world: to be at Timewells. And – however angry they all were, when the truth came out – Mum would have had her holiday first. And so would she.

The more she thought about it, the better this plan seemed. And another thing: she needn't walk all the way. She could take the train on to Chichester, this evening, and walk from there.

But not yet ... she needn't leave here till the light began to fade. Outside, it was still brilliant day, blue and gold and green. She went on gazing.

The train put her down at dusk on Chichester station. Coming into the air, she found herself shivering. A long way to go, still: and – she couldn't help guessing – of all the things that had happened today, this long night walk by herself would be the one that Dad and Mum would hate most.

And yet – what could she do? She *must* get home. There wasn't a bus as late as this.

Walking past a row of taxis, she thought, If only I had enough money, I could take one of those. How lovely, just to get in and be whirled off to Timewells. Like that Friday when we came down alone, Ned and Karen and Berry and me, because Dad and Mum had to stay in town till late.

One taxi had a lighted sign with the name of the firm. She remembered – that was the one we took. How much did it cost? Ned must have paid the driver.

Then it came to her – no, he didn't. He'd told the man – something like – "Our name's Buckley, my father has an accountant with you." No, that wasn't the right word. An account, that was it – meaning Dad would pay the fare later.

Arabella stood still. Then, before she could change her mind, she turned and walked back to the taxi. A girl was sitting in the driver's seat, reading a newspaper. No one she knew . . . Arabella stepped up to the window.

"Please – "

She put down the paper.

"Please – could you take me out to Timewells, at Timber? I – we – the Buckleys have an account with you – "

It all came out in a breathless rush; and she waited, quaking. Suppose the girl said, "Hello, Arabella Buckley. Why aren't you in France?"

But she didn't. She said, "Sure," and leaned back to open the rear door. Sliding into warm leather-smelling darkness, Arabella heard her say something into her radio. *Timewells*, yes; and *Buckleys*. The pause seemed to last for hours. Then a loud cheerful voice spoke from the other end. It said:

"OK, darling."

Arabella sank back against the cushions. She felt immensely comforted: as though, for the first time since she woke that morning, she was really doing something right and sensible.

Darling drove away through the streets and into the open country: heading for the downs, the dark beech-woods and home.

Then they were in the lane outside the cottage. Arabella jumped out: the girl nodded goodnight. The taxi turned, sweeping a great arc of light through the trees, over the field where Baggins lived.

She saw him standing there by the fence, ears pricked: just as though he'd known she was coming. She went over and put her arms round his neck. It was by far the best moment of the day.

6

Coming home

The garden at Timewells felt like part of the cottage; a warm quiet room with old brick walls, the colour of raw carrot, and the sky for a ceiling, arching over from tree to tree.

As soon as she slipped through the door, and heard it go *chock* in the wall behind her, she felt she was really home.

She stood there in the dusk, breathing in the summer smells, catmint, thyme, lavender and the velvet warmth of snapdragons. Then she made her way to the stable-yard.

The smells here were different: horse-radish leaves and stinging nettles. These nettles were such old enemies, they almost felt like friends. One of them got her on the ankle, as usual, while she was groping along the wall with her finger-tips, feeling for the loose brick. She prized out the brick, and behind it was the secret key, that only the family knew about.

Her feet knew every inch of the path to the front door. She stepped over mats of wild thyme and tendrils of Alpine strawberries. Stooping, she found one of the little strawberries and put it in her mouth. It melted on her tongue like an acid-drop.

She unlocked the front door, and shut it without a sound. The deep shadows of indoors seemed to fold her round. She thought – I'm *here*. I've done it. I'm home.

The silence was full of friendly voices, little squeaks and

creaks, the tick of the grandfather clock, the rustle of a moth in a window pane. She tiptoed into the kitchen.

All day she'd been far too excited to eat anything but a biscuit or two from her pack. Now suddenly she was starving.

The fridge would be empty, having its weekday rest. She crossed to the old cottage larder. It was cool as a church in there, the slate shelves packed with stores. She shone her torch along them. Jars of paste, a whole row of them, and cans of fruit juice, and that thick sticky milk . . . biscuits . . . butter . . . cheese . . . cornflakes. Bottles of squash. Three eggs in the rack. Potatoes in the bin. She could have fried eggs, lovely, and instant coffee.

And in the back kitchen there was the freezer, with enough ice-cream and sausages and chicken wings to last for weeks.

She switched on the electric stove, and a hot-plate, and took the frying-pan off its hook. She was just going to put some butter in the pan – when a new thought struck her.

Mrs Hat. She'd be coming in tomorrow, on the daily visit. She'd know someone had been here. When you fried eggs and made coffee, the kitchen was filled with cooking smells. In London, you got rid of those with the fresh-air fan; but there wasn't any fan at Timewells.

Here, you opened the kitchen windows and the fresh air poured in, blowing over the fields, straight from the sea. But she mustn't start opening windows. If someone came, there wouldn't be time to shut them again.

Would anyone really come, as late as this?

Yes: the policeman might. Dad said he sometimes checked the cottage, when they were away. The very last person she wanted to find her!

Boiled eggs, then . . . no smell, and no mess either. Biscuits with them, and butter. Lemon squash to drink. A midnight feast.

It was queer, finding things in the dark; and the pan of water took ages to boil; and she wasn't sure how long the eggs should be left in. They were runny, in the end; but she was too hungry to care. She ate a whole packet of biscuits, and found a carton of dried apricots to go with them.

Bed, now. She was so sleepy, she felt she could hardly walk upstairs. Oh, but the washing-up! That had to be done first, Mrs Hat mustn't find eggy things on the table . . . the egg-spoon was the worst, with only cold water to help; but it was done at last, and put away, and the egg-cup and butter-knife.

Upstairs, in the little room she shared with Karen, she took her teddy-bear off the lower bunk and put him on the top one. It was Karen's turn to sleep up there; but Karen was hundreds of miles away . . . She rushed into pyjamas, and climbed up beside him.

You heard of people falling asleep "as soon as their heads touched the pillow". That was what she was going to do.

And in the morning she could sleep and sleep, with no one to call her. Breakfast any time she liked. Lovely Timewells . . .

But then – just as she was drifting off to sleep – a frightening thought came. She sprang up in panic.

Suppose she overslept? Suppose Mrs Hat came early and found her?

She must wake earlier still, and hide. Where? Quickly she thought about her secret hiding-places; the walnut tree, the stable loft, the roof?

Then it came to her: of course, she needn't go out of doors to hide. There was the attic. Ned's room. She'd be safe up there, with the bolt across: Ned had fixed that to keep out intruders. He might not be pleased, when he knew she'd been in there; but anything was better than

37

being found out, and spoiling Mum's holiday. He'd said so himself.

She slid down from the bunk, remembered to smooth the bedclothes, and put Bear back on the lower bunk. She'd have liked to have him with her in the attic, for company; but Mrs Hat might remember he'd been here.

Shining her torch on the attic ladder, she saw the white gleam of a notice Ned had pinned on the trap-door, when he took over the attic. The lettering said: Ned's. No Entry. No Way.

She pushed at the trap-door, got it open, climbed through into the long low room under the roof, and slid the bolt inside. Now she felt safe.

But – suppose Mrs Hat came up the ladder and found the door bolted? Well, she could unbolt it in the morning, and hide somewhere – behind the water tank, yes! Mrs Hat was large and plump; she wouldn't do more than stick her head through the trap to see that all was well?

Arabella looked about eagerly. The attic had once been a favourite rainy-day place of hers: snug and secretive, smelling of dust and apples, dimly lit by a skylight.

This was only the second time she'd been up here since Ned moved in. He'd allowed them all just one brief visit to admire the improvements, a special present from Dad and Mum. Now there was a casement window at each end, as well as a fitted basin, heater and electric kettle. Ned had chosen some bits of furniture and fixed up a painting-table. It all smelled of whitewash, new matting, coffee, oranges and turps.

Super, she thought. I'll settle in here, and only go downstairs when there's no one about.

She opened the window at the far end; even by day, that wouldn't be seen from below, because of the chimney stack.

A new scent drifted in, from the tassel flowers on the

Spanish chestnut tree. She took a deep breath. That smell, sweet and heavy, always meant the start of the summer holidays.

A sneeze began in the back of her nose. She groped for a hanky. It *had* been in her pocket – she'd wiped her fingers on it, after those dried apricots . . . but it wasn't there now. Bother. Suppose she'd dropped it downstairs?

She ran her torch over the floor, then drew back the bolt and searched the ladder, the landing, the stairs . . . here it was! On the bottom stair. Mrs Hat would have known that wasn't there before. What luck, to have found it before she did.

But it was all being much harder than she'd realized, just to stop people from guessing anyone was here. What other clues could she have forgotten? She began to check, from the front door on.

Oh heavens – she'd left the secret key in the outside lock! Fool, fool. And her pack, still on the mat where she'd dropped it! Biscuit crumbs on the kitchen table. Rubbish in the bucket – tossed there without thinking. A *damp* tea-towel on the rail. The switch above the stove still showing ON.

She'd have to do a whole lot better than this. But never mind; she'd thought of everything this time, she was certain. She found a plastic bag, swept crumbs and litter and tea-towel into it and carried them with her, back to the attic.

The sounds were different up here. She lay listening, curled under Ned's duvet. That faint hissing . . . no, it wasn't snakes, it came from the water pipes. And that gentle *dank-a-dank* was only the tank in the corner. But there was something else: not inside, but out there in the dark. A sort of twittering.

What was it ghosts were supposed to do? Oh yes, they *gibbered*.

She put her head under the duvet. The twittering seemed to come too. She sat up, and it faded away for a moment, then began again.

Suddenly there was a swish of wings. The tiny sounds swelled to a cheeping chattering chorus. A bird hovered, crying *Twit, twit!* and flew upward, out of sight.

Twit, Arabella told herself. A swallow's nest, of course – they always built in the eaves. But she'd never known they worked so late, keeping their young ones fed.

Now the cheeping died away; the nestlings slept. The night was so still, she could hear the drowsy sound of the stream in the far meadows. The swallows' long day was over. So, at last, was Arabella's.

7

A card to Christchurch

Before it was light the parent swallows were out and away, after gnats and midges. Arabella stirred, and remembered with triumph that she was here, not in France . . . Geese in the farmyard were honking and croaking. She slept again, dreaming of giant frogs.

Waking properly, she lay and looked round the attic. Ned had whitewashed the walls and pinned up paintings and posters, and postcard views of Sauterelle. There was a striking portrait, stretching from floor to ceiling, done in brown chalk on bright yellow paper. A face, sideways. Just a few lines, an eyebrow, a tiny nose, a curve of hair – but you could *see* Chantal.

A calendar hung on the wall by her pillow. Today's date, Saturday the 21st July, was outlined with scarlet ink, and ringed in gold stars. Today, he'd be seeing her again. Chantal herself, not just a painting or a photograph.

It seemed wrong to know so much about the way Ned felt. No wonder he didn't want anyone else in here. She got up quickly. Breakfast. She'd carry everything up from the kitchen, and have it in the window, near the young swallows.

Down in the kitchen she found cornflakes, a tin of milk, brown sugar, crispbread, butter, and dumped them all into a bin-liner. She was hunting round for a pot of honey when a sound made her gasp and jump.

The thud of the garden door. Footsteps on the path. Mrs Hat already? She fled upstairs.

From the attic steps, she heard the rattle of the letter-box, and a light flutter as something came through. So it had only been a postman, after all.

She waited to hear the van drive off, then stole down again. A postcard lay on the mat. "The beach at Bude." The writing said, "Happy holidays to you all. Best love, Auntie Erica."

She pinned it up with Ned's postcards, and ate her cornflakes, smiling to herself.

Auntie Erica was often late off the mark. Her Christmas cards were apt to arrive about St Valentine's Day. At half-term in summer, with the garden full of roses and fox-gloves, you'd get a "Happy Easter" card, all lambs and daffodils. This card should have come last weekend – so she'd really done quite well: only a week adrift.

Today, Arabella remembered, the others would be sending off cards to Dad and Mum. She must send one too, or they'd think it odd. Bright idea – she'd send one of Ned's, off the wall. A view of Sauterelle. Ned was sure to bring back some more.

She chose one with dark blue sea, red and yellow striped awnings, beach mats; and nipped out the drawing-pins. Ned had left a biro on the table. She wrote, after careful thought:

"Good journey here." (Well, it had been.) "Enjoying it so far." (She mustn't sound too enthusiastic.) "Hope you're having a super time." (And, she thought, I hope you'll go on doing that, with no worries about Arabella.) "Thank you for your letter." That was enough about *that*.

She addressed it to Uncle Hugh's house in Christchurch. Now a stamp – there'd be some in the desk downstairs.

She found a sheet of first-class stamps. Would one be enough for New Zealand? Better put two to make sure.

She was just going to lick them – when it dawned on her: the card should have French stamps! And the postmark – it ought to say "Sauterelle", not "Sussex Coast"! All wrong again. The card couldn't go.

But it ought to go. Dad and Mum would think she'd forgotten. Or, much worse, they might think she was sulking.

She fiddled gloomily with the things on the desk, biros, pencils, sellotape, another postcard, the Bluebell Railway. She changed the driver into a mouse, with a brown biro, and wished she could send it to Berry.

But of course she could!

She almost laughed aloud – that was the answer! She'd simply put the Railway card in an envelope, and address it to Berry, and enclose the one for New Zealand, and tell Berry to post it for her. Ginette would give him the right stamp. No one would think it odd. Ever since Berry had started his postman craze, they'd all been giving him letters to post.

The Sussex postmark wouldn't matter – *they* knew she was here. And the one for New Zealand would be all right too.

She printed her message for Berry – "Don't you wish you were here?" – and sealed the two cards in an envelope, and wrote, "Berry Buckley, c/o Madame Rosier, Mas des Roses, Sauterelle, France." I'll go out after dark and post it, she thought, and it'll go first thing on Monday.

For a moment she felt pleased with herself.

Then she began to wonder – what will the others say in their cards? Suppose Karen puts – "Arab was over the moon about going to Timewells"? And Ginette! – she was sure to write too. And she couldn't help saying something about the change of plan.

No good worrying, though. She'd done all she could for the moment. Even if it all came out, and Ginette arrived to fetch her – even then, she'd have had a few days at Timewells.

She got into comfortable old clothes – jeans and shirt passed on from Karen, grubby old trainers – and tipped her pack out on to the attic floor. Cool cotton shirts with long sleeves, trousers to match, bought specially for the holiday – she wouldn't want those now. They could go in Ned's cupboard . . . *what was that?*

Voices, down in the garden. Someone was coming.

She lay with her ear to the trap-door, listening. Mrs Hat, yes – and someone with her. Randal, her son – Ran, his mother called him. An odd quiet boy – she'd never seen much of him. He seemed to hate them all, and he kept out of their way. Even at the riding-school, where he and she sometimes met, cleaning tack or mucking out together – you'd hardly get a word out of him.

He sounded chatty enough now – calling out to his mother as he opened windows downstairs. In a minute he'd be coming up . . . oh but – suppose he came right up to the attic? *He* could get through the trap easily enough! She must hide, quickly.

In frantic haste she grabbed the pack, the rubbish-bag, the bin-liner, and pushed them under the couch. Then she climbed through the window, pressing it shut behind her. She was out on the leads, a narrow flat strip between two slopes of the kitchen roof. She crawled along, and tucked herself out of sight behind the high chimney.

Safe. And she'd covered her tracks so well, after those first silly mistakes – they'd never guess that anyone had set foot in the place.

8

Something there

The moment Ran came through the door, he knew the house was different.

He stood still by the stairs and looked around, thinking – *What is it?* Nothing to see or hear . . . it was more a *feeling*. Timewells didn't seem empty any more. "Something there" was the nearest he could get. He'd never felt that before, indoors. (The garden was another matter – something *there* all right.)

He went from room to room, opening windows to let in the air. His mother was plugging in the sweeper for her Saturday "do round". She hadn't noticed anything . . . well, was there really anything to notice? Nothing had changed since yesterday, so far as he could see.

Yes: one thing. Up in the girls' room, the old teddy-bear had flopped sideways on the pillow. Yesterday, he'd been sitting up straight.

What had made him fall over suddenly? He'd never done it before.

Traffic in the lane outside? That could shake the cottage – as it sometimes shook their own place, higher up the lane. A harvester going by, perhaps; or a big horse-box on its way to the races? A helicopter, even, flying low. Something like that.

He set Bear upright, and sat down on the bunk, gazing at him thoughtfully. Glass eyes, brown as toffee, looked

45

back at him kindly from the worn yellow face. Ran found himself whispering:

"Go on, old bear. Tell."

For a moment he almost thought it might speak, and tell him . . . well, something. Then he laughed at himself, and cuffed Bear lightly, and stroked his ears. He muttered, "All right then. Keep it to yourself. You're not the only one."

The only one with a secret, he meant.

Ran had kept his own secret for years; ever since he and his mother came to live next door. He pretended to himself that he was one of the Buckley family. He'd always wanted brothers and sisters. And he was just the right age – he fitted in nicely between Karen and Arabella.

At first, he used to lurk about in hiding, watching and listening, pretending to be part of their games. He soon realized that, if he'd shown himself, they would really have let him play with them; but he was far too shy – and then it seemed far too late. They'd all grown used to his scowling when they met, or running past with a muttered "Hello".

Later, like Arabella, he began to save his pocket-money for riding lessons at the school a few miles away. Now he spent all his spare time there, helping with the chores. He still couldn't make himself talk to her – but at least they were doing the same thing.

Berry was the only one he could talk to. When the others were out of the way, Ran showed him birds' nests or gave him bike rides.

He also knew a lot about Ned and Karen. Sometimes his mother sent him up to check the attic, just in case squatters had got in; and he couldn't help looking at Ned's things. Also, he had noticed when Karen stopped being keen on ballet and started practising to be a gymnast. He watched her walking along the tops of fences, and trying to do back flips. No one else had guessed about this.

It was a blow when they went away for two weeks, last summer. And much worse now, when they'd be gone for a month. A waste of the holidays, he thought – and he knew Arabella thought so too. He kept an eye on Baggins for her, riding him in the field and bringing him titbits.

Looking after Timewells helped, too: he came in most days with his mother. He could pretend he lived here, and that he'd stayed behind on purpose, because that was the way he liked it.

But, today – he had this odd feeling about the place. As though someone had been about. But not burglars or intruders – nothing unfriendly . . .

All the same, as he wandered round, he found things that puzzled him. A faint scrunching when he walked across the kitchen floor. He ran a finger-tip over it. Sugar: a few spilt grains. And a crumb of cornflake. A scrap of stamp-paper by the desk in the sitting-room. A sticky mark on the stair-rail. Had they been there yesterday? And the day before?

No one could get in by the front door – the key never left his mother's handbag. What about the windows? He checked them again. No broken panes – and the catches seemed just as usual. No footprints on the sills, either. Surely no one could come down a chimney?

But it was the passage by the front door that made him feel really uneasy. Something was wrong there, he felt certain – something *missing* – yet he couldn't think what it might be.

He wanted to stay here, and go on trying to puzzle it out. But he'd promised to help at the riding-school, getting ready for gymkhana practice.

All that afternoon, while he worked at the new jumps, and knocked in posts for bending – somehow he couldn't get the cottage out of his mind.

47

9

Timewells

When the Hats were gone, Arabella danced on the roof from sheer joy and relief. She was all right, now, till tomorrow. A whole day to herself – a whole house to herself. The mistress of the house.

To celebrate, she plugged in Ned's kettle and made tea. Mum always did that, the minute they arrived here.

The tea looked a bit weird when she poured it out: pale, with black sprigs floating. But it tasted fine. The first she'd ever made by herself: till now, there had always been someone *older* to do things like that.

She climbed through the window again and sat on the leads, sipping blissfully.

It was a soft sunny morning with a faint breeze. The swallows went on flitting to and fro. She could see a ring of glossy heads on the rim of the nest. The harvester hummed in the distance. A kestrel hovered, watching for mice in the wheat-field. Far above it, swifts wheeled and dived, black crescent shapes against the sky.

Suddenly all the birds disappeared. A helicopter came buzzing over. Arabella stood up and waved, in case the Prince of Wales was in it. Then she sat down in the shadow of the chimney stack, bare feet on the warm tiles.

She didn't feel lonely today; and she wasn't missing the others. In a way, they seemed to be here too. And another thing: she didn't feel like an outlaw any more. She'd been

48

born in this cottage – perhaps that was why. I belong here, she thought.

You weren't an outlaw in your own place. Of course, you could still be a prisoner, a fugitive. Like the Cavaliers sometimes. Or like that Frenchman who hid in his country home all through the Revolution, and afterwards – watching the swallows come and go, year after year . . . he'd put a ring on one of them, to prove that the same birds came back . . . days and years, watching swallows . . . his enemies never found him . . .

She drowsed off, and woke when a swallow dipped over her with its twittering call. Lovely just to sit here. She'd had such a scramble, yesterday, getting to Timewells.

Timewells. She felt she'd never understood the name until now. At Sauterelle she'd been a fish out of water. Here she was in water; deep, deep wells of time, to spend as she liked.

Of course, she must stay invisible – like a ghost, in a way. Perhaps there were ghosts here all the time. Perhaps the eggler's daughters came back sometimes: it had been their home too. They'd lived here a hundred years ago, a father and mother and three girls. Dad had found that out from some old records.

The father was an eggler, an egg-seller. He kept a pony and cart, and went about buying eggs from the farmers and selling them at the market. When she and Karen had been younger they'd played at eggling, with snowberries and brown acorns for eggs.

In broad daylight, with the sun shining, she didn't mind thinking about ghosts. But now she felt wide awake again. She fetched *The Hobbit* from Ned's shelf and read for a bit, but she didn't get far. All the feasting in the first chapter soon made it seem like dinner-time.

Downstairs, she looked wistfully at tins of this and that in the larder. No use, she knew. She just wasn't any good with tin-openers – it was all she could do to spike a tin of milk. No beans for her, then, or grapefruit, or creamed chicken. But there was plenty of shrimp paste, in those sensible screw-top jars. Biscuits, to spread it on. Crisps. A can of orange juice, that opened when you simply pulled a tag. Ice-cream out of the freezer . . . She carried it all up to the roof, and took out Ned's duvet and pillow to laze on.

One thought began to worry her: how soon would Mrs Hat notice that the stores were disappearing?

She *could* put back the empty packets . . . but then Mrs Hat might lift them, to dust or something – and she'd find out that way.

It did need thinking about. Perhaps she could go to some shop, a long way off, and buy stuff with her holiday money.

Not today, though. Today was a real holiday. Posting the letter to Berry would be tricky enough – she'd have to stay awake till dark, and steal out when people were in bed. And this was Saturday, when a lot of them stayed up late. Never mind; the sun was still high overhead. Time enough to think about the letter, when it was over in the west, behind the steep beechwood called Squerries.

But the afternoon flew past. Supper-time already.

One egg left. She could have that boiled, like last night's. Boiled potatoes didn't leave any smell either. They were new potatoes; the skin peeled off like sunburn when she scrubbed them. She spun out supper as long as possible.

The west side of the attic was filled with sunlight. Slowly the sun disappeared behind the beeches. Sunset, and then twilight . . . soon, now, she could go.

She sat watching for the first stars. Then she thought she might as well lie on the couch. Mustn't fall asleep . . . but if she shut her eyes, just for a minute, and then opened them – the dark would come more quickly. She shut her eyes.

And sat up, gasping.

What had happened? Where was this?

Oh yes – the attic, of course. She'd been waiting to post that letter. She must have slept for ages. Quick now . . . but where *was* the letter? She'd put it under the pillow. It must have fallen to the floor. Or had she got it out already, and left it somewhere else? On the table? The shelf?

She groped about in panic, and couldn't find it. She'd have to use her torch. Just one flash, and then switch off – no one would notice that. The village must be asleep . . . She shone the torch on and off, three times, and still couldn't see the letter. Growing reckless, she shone it for several moments. Here was the letter! It had slipped down the back of the couch.

She wriggled into her thick sweater, and began to lace her shoes.

A distant sound made her stop to listen. A drumming noise. A motor-bike, on the main road. Yes, and more than one. Coming nearer, louder. She ran to the window. Lights flashed in the distance – headlamps – and then they were in the village: a whole troop of motor-bikes, going full tilt, roaring along the street. Past the church – and, yes – they were turning down here, coming down the lane! The noise was deafening.

She held her breath as they zoomed past, trying to count. Ten . . . fourteen . . . still coming. Poor Baggins, he'd be scared. He hated motor-bikes.

They were gone, howling away past the cross-roads. A hush fell. But no – more of them were on the way, roaring along the road, along the street, down the lane, past and gone – and back again, and again. The same gang, circling round and round.

She saw a light go on over in the farmhouse ... then they were back for the fifth time.

She remembered hearing that this had happened once before, when the Buckleys were in London. A teenage gang from along the coast, Mrs Hat said: out for trouble, stirring up the village lads.

Sirens now, far away: someone had rung the police.

But the gang had really gone this time. A police car hummed past down the lane, blue light flashing; and that was the last sound she heard. Now the night was quiet again.

She mustn't go out yet, though. They might still come back – or that police car might. She didn't want to meet any of them.

She sat for a long time, shivering and wide awake, determined to get the letter on its way.

When she thought the silence had lasted long enough, she slid off the window-seat and picked up the letter once more.

An ancient anorak, dark with age, hung on a peg: just the thing, she thought. Her fawn-coloured sweater would show up in the dark. She huddled into the anorak, pulled up the hood and zipped the letter firmly into one of the pockets. Sugar lumps in the other, for Baggins. Now.

She knelt, drew back the bolt, and tugged. The door came up quietly.

Then she shrieked aloud in fear, and let the trap-door fall.

10

A light in the attic

Ran bicycled home from the riding-school, still thinking about Timewells. Should he go in there tonight, and have another look round? He felt he couldn't bear to wait till tomorrow.

At home, he managed to filch the key, while his mother's back was turned.

After she'd gone to bed, he got up, pulled on a jersey and stole out on to the landing. Her light was still on, the door ajar. He moved carefully past: too carefully, a floorboard squeaked, and she called:

"What's wrong?"

"Just – getting a drink."

"Come in here . . . I thought as much. Why have you got that jersey on? Where are you off to?"

"Baggins. Forgot to give him his sugar . . ."

"Nonsense. Tomorrow will do. Sugar, indeed!"

"Oh Mum – shan't be a minute. Promised Arabella – "

"H'm. Well – come straight back in, do you hear? And" – she raised her voice as he sped downstairs – "No going off with those gangs, either. I'll give *you* sugar if you do!"

"Oh Mum," he laughed from the foot of the stairs. "What gangs?"

In fact there were several gangs in the village; but he didn't belong to any of them. Arabella was right, he thought: ponies were a lot more fun.

He coaxed Baggins to the fence and sat there, patting him and doling out sugar lumps. All the time, his eyes were on the dark cottage over the wall; so were his thoughts. Baggins knew that, and nipped his shoulder in reproach.

At the same moment, Ran gasped and jumped, nearly falling off the rail. Not because of the nip. He thought he'd seen something over there – a faint gleam, lighting up the beech leaves.

It had vanished at once – but, *there* – it came again. A kind of glow, wandering about in the attic.

A cold tingle, like a raindrop, seemed to touch the back of his neck and run down his spine: an icy shiver. And then he saw it for the third time – a faint, faint shining that jigged for a second and went out.

He waited, clutching Baggins for company; and the gleam returned. This time there was no mistake. He *was* seeing something, behind the dark attic window. An eerie glimmer, greenish, like a cat's eyes – though that might be the green of the leaves as it shone through.

Gone again.

The word *spectre* came into his mind; and his heart beat fast. Was Timewells really haunted – inside, as well as out? But, he thought, *night ghosts* belonged to winter-time. Autumn, anyway; with firelight, and moaning winds, and dead leaves tapping on window panes. Not light summer nights like this, smelling of flowers and straw.

But then – if it wasn't a ghost – someone was up there. And he had to do something about it. He and his mother were the caretakers.

He slid off the fence and stood still. Should he run home and tell Mum about the light? She'd have the police there in no time. But – suppose there was nothing, after all? Suppose he'd made a mistake? They'd laugh at him, and say he'd been dreaming.

He didn't like this idea at all.

His hand went into his jersey pocket, fingering the key. He'd meant to go in there, all along – and now he *must* go, and see for himself, before he did anything else. Yes: that would be far the best.

He had just made up his mind – when he found that something else was happening. The night wasn't quiet any longer. A roaring sounded in the distance. Motor-bikes, going full tilt, through the village – *coming here*. He dived over the fence and took cover, just as the first flashed by, followed by twenty more. Not the village gang, he saw . . . they were circling, coming back . . .

Baggins had long ago raced, snorting, to the far side of the field. Ran stood behind a clump of gorse: just as well not to show yourself, when a rag like this was on. He didn't fancy being taken prisoner.

They made five deafening circuits. In between, he heard shouts from the farmhouse – that would be the farmer, saying what he thought of them. Ran grinned to himself. Another time round? No, the noise had really died away this time. Police sirens, now. He waited, and saw the patrol car slide past down the lane.

And then, in a flash, it came to him: the thing that had puzzled him all day.

This morning, at breakfast, he'd heard another car go down the lane. The post van. It had gone past their cottage, and stopped at Timewells. He'd heard the sound of the garden door, twice. Then it had driven off.

The postman had left a letter at Timewells. But there hadn't been any letter. *That* was what had been missing, by the front door. He'd known there was something wrong; now he knew what it was. Someone had got in there somehow – how? – and taken the letter.

A ghost wouldn't do that. Someone *was* in there . . . all the same, he was going to have a look for himself. Quick, now, before he could change his mind or start to lose his nerve.

He climbed the beech tree, dropped into the garden and crept to the front door. All seemed quiet. No lights now. He turned the key in the latch, opened the door a crack, slipped through and left it unlatched, ready for retreat.

He was standing on the mat where the letter should have been this morning. He knelt and groped about, to make sure. Nothing there. He stood up again, and listened, holding his breath.

Nothing to hear; only his own heart thumping. Nothing to see: his eyes strained through the darkness. But, again, there was that queer sense of *something there*. He knew he wasn't alone in the house. And – wasn't there a faint warm smell of cooking? Like beans, perhaps. Or potatoes?

He began to creep upstairs, one step at a time, dodging the creaks. He came to the landing, and waited, shivering. Still no sound from any of the rooms; no movement. But that light had been up in the attic: that was where they were hiding.

He got to the ladder, put his foot on the lowest rung and began to climb. Slowly, slowly, he came near the trap-door, put up his hand and gave it a tiny shove. It didn't move.

It was bolted, inside.

He took his hand away and slid down to the landing. Now he'd done enough – he must dash home and tell his mother.

Then, at last, he did hear something. Faint sounds overhead. Footsteps, padding across the floor. Oh, but so light and quiet – it was like the tread of a cat. Ran hesitated, listening; and all his doubts came back. That greenish gleam – *was* it just a cat, after all? But cats didn't steal letters.

Then he caught his breath. The trap-door was opening slowly.

He couldn't move: he stood frozen, looking up. Something crouched up there, all in black. Smallish, he thought – no bigger than himself –

Then came the shriek.

The door crashed shut, the bolt rattled across. Ran found himself hurtling downstairs, tearing through the garden and up the lane; back indoors, and up to his own room.

His mother called out to him, talking about the motorbike gang, scolding him for being so long. He answered somehow, and shut his bedroom door and tumbled into bed. He lay there panting, and whispered to himself –

"But it was a kid. Just a kid. And scared. *So what do I do now?*"

A kid . . . that would explain the teddy-bear . . . but who, and where from, and how in the world did it get in? And *why*?

Suppose someone else had been up there? A grown-up person?

No . . . the shriek echoed in his mind. He'd given it such a fright – it would have called out, if there'd been anyone else there to call to. He felt quite sure of that. But after the shriek – he'd heard nothing. Not a sound. Only the slam of the trap-door, and the noise of the bolt. Suppose it had fainted from sheer terror?

If only he hadn't run away . . . But somehow he couldn't help it. The shriek had given *him* such a fright – as though *he* were a panicky kid as well, not a proper caretaker doing his job . . .

Tossing about, waiting for dawn, he told himself: you know what? The minute it starts to get light, you're going back.

11

A fright in the garden

Arabella shot the trap-door bolt and huddled there, shuddering from head to foot. Her own scream rang in her ears. But for that echo, the night was now utterly still.

It was one thing to wonder about ghosts, in a light-hearted way, by daylight – but quite another to find one lying in wait in the dark. That had been a fearful shock: lifting up the trap-door, thinking it was all right to go out – and then seeing *it* down there. A white face, floating out of shadows.

She could hardly bear to think of it; yet she couldn't think of anything else.

She wouldn't be able to lift that trap-door, ever again. From now on she'd have to go in and out by the roof and the chestnut tree.

Not tonight, though.

Anyway, she was bolted in safely.

But no! – ghosts didn't care about bolts or locks, they could float through doors, or through walls . . .

She backed away across the attic, fell on to the couch and hid under the duvet again. How silly to have been scared by swallows, last night! This was really frightening. If she looked out, she might see a ghastly, ghostly shape – *above* the door, this time.

At last she dared to take a stealthy look. Nothing there, after all. The attic seemed quite peaceful. A star winked in at her; the picture of Chantal glimmered on the wall. Ned could lie here and look at her . . .

She thought she would never go to sleep again. But somehow – in a moment, it seemed – it was morning. Not pale early dawn, but bright day, with the sun high, and the church bell ringing, out beyond the stable-yard, for early service. It was so quiet that she thought she could hear the creak of the bell-rope in the church tower.

Sunday morning . . . she felt rested, and hungry, and inclined to laugh – a bit shakily – about what she'd seen on the landing last night. Still – she was glad she'd brought the teapot and other breakfast things up here. No need to brave the trap-door *yet*, anyway.

The tea she made looked like proper tea, this time; she was quite proud of it. Munching cornflakes, she studied a picture on the back of the packet; a cut-out mask, a green goblin. She might make that some time for Berry.

This was going to be another hot day. Early mist hung over Squerries Wood. Already, when she went to sit out-side, the roof felt warm underfoot.

And the greenfinches were back – a flock of them, tril-ling and calling in the apple trees. They came every year, in the first week of the summer holidays.

Earlier, in April, a pair would nest at the wild end of the garden. Once, she'd tried making a nest ready for them, but it didn't work: she couldn't make all those roots and twigs stick together at all. How did *they* manage, with only their beaks to do it?

On days like this, when they were younger, she and Karen used to have picnics down there, with apple-leaf plates and black-currant tea. The guests would be poppy-head dolls in white sun-hats – bindweed flowers – and red petal skirts. They used to wonder if the eggler's children had played the same games.

She longed to be down in the garden now. Well – why

not? If the Hats came, she could hide in the bushes. She'd take the bag with the egg-shells and potato skins, and bury all that, and fill the bag with things from the garden.

She listened carefully before she swung into the chestnut tree and dropped to the path; then she crossed the garden warily, zig-zag: one eye on the door, the other on the wasps' nest in the wall. Dad said the wasps wouldn't sting, unless you got in their flight-path and exasperated them.

It was lovely down here, after being cooped up in the attic. She hid the rubbish in the rhubarb bed, and picked a rhubarb stick to chew, and then a lot of honeysuckles to take away the sourness. Each had a single drop of nectar, corked in by a green cap. She chose a little of everything to go in the bag: a late apricot, an early apple, a handful of cherry-plums, another of Alpine strawberries; radishes, a lettuce, a carrot or two, a pinch of mint to sniff, a sprig of sorrel to nibble at.

A grasshopper was rasping away on the little lawn. She stalked it, and touched it with a blade of grass to see how far it could jump.

In the lupin bed she tapped the ripe black seed-pods to hear them crack open with a sound like tiny pistol shots.

A slim brown lizard was sunning itself on the wall. As she came near, it slid into a crevice. She put in a finger to stroke it, but the crack was too deep, she couldn't even touch its tail. Her finger-tip found something else, and she fished it out. A cockleshell.

Another of those shells! The garden was full of them, cockles and scallops and oyster-shells, grey and crumbly, and mussels, dark and brittle with age. They turned up in odd places, tree-holes, cracks and crannies, as though they'd been hidden in some game, or tucked away like a squirrel's hoard.

She turned it over. On the inside, you could just make

out the faint outline of a capital letter, scratched with a pin or a pen-nib. An A.

Another A . . . she'd found a lot of those. Sometimes a J.

Arabella wandered down to the wild end of the garden, and sat on a tree-stump, twirling the shell on her finger-tip. Again – as so often, out here – she found herself thinking about the eggler's children. Their name was Shelley. A good Sussex name, Dad said: the poet Shelley had been born in Sussex too.

Had *they* marked the shells, and used them in their games, for counters perhaps – and hidden them, as tokens – because of their name? One of them was called Jane, so the J could be hers. But the others were Eliza and Mary Ellen. Then who had marked all these A's?

She was sitting there so quietly that a wood mouse crept out and ran up a foxglove stalk. His footsteps shook the stalk, and a seed-pod burst, showering him with brown dust like sneezing-powder. He squeaked and bolted: just in time, she stopped herself from laughing out loud.

The foxgloves were over, all but one or two pinkish bells. Summer went far too quickly always. There was a dead leaf already, caught up on a bush.

But no – it wasn't a leaf. She looked closer. It was a brown moth, a huge one, clinging to a twig. She blew softly, and the wings quivered and spread wide. Arabella almost cried out in surprise. She'd never seen a moth like this: almost as big as a wren, with striped wings, foxglove-pink and nut-brown, and soft brown fur at the back of its head. She breathed, "Oh . . ." and the fur rippled as though a breeze had stirred it.

She was so intent on the moth that she didn't hear voices in the lane, and running footsteps.

The sudden bang of the garden door made her jump and catch her breath. She crouched in the bushes, listening. Not the Hats. She peered through the leaves, and her heart

61

sank. Two small boys were darting about the garden. One ran to knock on the front door. The other shouted:

"I told you! He's not here!"

She knew them, of course – two of Berry's friends, Rob and Nick. They were well named: they raced to the plum tree, snatching and gobbling, pelting each other with the stones.

Could she get to the chestnut tree, and climb up, while they were busy? No, too risky. Those imps wouldn't stay in the same place more than half a minute. Panic swept over her. She was trapped.

If they did see her, it would be all over the village in an hour or so. Unless – could she *bribe* them not to tell? No: that wouldn't be any good. You might as well try bribing two sparrows not to chirp. If only they didn't come down here . . .

Rob was running a toy car up and down the brick path, with a live white mouse as passenger. Nick was stuffing his pockets with cherry-plums, first taking out a grass-snake which he dropped inside his T-shirt. Now they were at the swing, scuffling for first turn, then swinging together.

Arabella began edging along the path the other way, till she reached the shelter of a mulberry tree that hung down like a tent. Now she was too near the wasps' nest for comfort, but that couldn't be helped. Looking out, she saw the swing spinning, empty. Where had they got to?

They came into sight again, running over the lawn, brandishing two sticks and having a sword-fight. Rob stopped suddenly, beating the air and shouting:

"Something's buzzed me! Wow! There it is again – "

"Wopses, wopses, all over the shopses," yelled Nick, dancing about, waving his stick. Then he pointed at the wall.

"Ooooh, look! In there – see? Hundreds of 'm. A nest – "

"Cor."

"Cor."

They rushed to the wall and stood on either side of the nest, exchanging a silent laughing look. She read their wicked thoughts: Shall we? Go on, then. No, you. I dare you. Well, I dare *you* . . . Rob took a step nearer, grasping the stick, his face alight with mischief. In a moment, he'd be stirring the nest: wasps would pour out in thousands, furious, murderous, mad for revenge.

But he mustn't! Arabella started up. They'd be stung to death – a miracle they hadn't been stung already, the fools, the little grinning idiots. Secret or no secret, she couldn't let that happen.

She opened her mouth to yell at the top of her voice: "STOP! STOP! GET AWAY FROM THERE!"

They yelped in alarm, skipping out of danger.

But she hadn't made a sound. It wasn't *her* voice. Someone had come in silently, and seen them, and shouted in the nick of time.

Ran Hat.

12

Meeting at dusk

Ran had had a dreadful morning. Everything had gone wrong.

How could he have dropped asleep like that, wrecking his plan to be up at first light? And then slept so late, till his mother called him to breakfast?

Then he simply couldn't get away. He was wanted for this job and that. Friends were coming for dinner, and to stay the night. Before that, there'd be church. But he *must* get to Timewells somehow.

At last he burst out, "Look, I'll check the cottage, shall I? Save you going – can't I? Go on, Mum, let me!"

Unwise to nag, he knew. But he saw her waver, thinking – mint sauce, salad, peel the eggs, skin the tomatoes, change my skirt, do my hair, *is that the time already?*

"Well – this once, then. Here's the key. Just have a good look round – come straight back, mind – "

So he arrived just in time to snatch Rob and Nick from disaster.

He hooked a finger and thumb around each of their necks, marched them over to the garden door, and hissed, "Now then! Which of you was it last night? Come on – were both of you up there?"

Blank looks of innocence. "What d'you mean, Ran? We wasn't anywhere – "

He shook them, and the white mouse and grass-snake

fell at their feet. Ran swooped and pocketed them: useful hostages...

But they went on protesting and denying; and he saw it must be true. He knew their parents, Rob's elder sister, Nick's watchful Granny. Whatever brat had been out of bed last night, trespassing in Timewells attic – it couldn't have been one of these. He'd have to accept that. Besides – the trespasser had looked bigger, now he came to think of it.

"Now listen. If I catch you here again, either of you, before Berry gets back – I'll loose that mouse in the wheat-field. You hear me? And I'll put your snake in the pond. Now buzz off."

He handed over the hostages. The pair grabbed them and fled, squeaking and giggling; stopping at a safe distance to chant, "Bandy Randy, he's got nits, can't catch me for toffee sticks."

Ran let himself into the cottage.

The clues were all here, as plain as day, now that he *knew*. Eggs gone from the larder, yes, and that cornflake packet with the goblin mask (the end packet had a lion mask now) and other stuff, he was certain.

He braced himself, and stole upstairs, and up the ladder. The trap-door was still bolted on the other side.

So the kid was still up there: wolfing eggs and cornflakes and whatever else it had nicked. The nerve of it! And what was he going to do? And how had it got in? By the roof, of course: that was the only way. Must have broken the attic window. He'd go up *now*, and see.

But, as he turned, the church bell began to ring. He must get along home, or Mum would be here after him. Was he going to tell her? Poor old Mum – it would spoil her day all right. *Need* he tell her? Surely he could handle a squatter that size! There'd be the window to mend, of course, but he thought he could fix that. He'd helped the

Rector with that broken pane in the vestry.

Closing the front door quietly, he decided – I can slip away after dinner, and climb up there, and take it by surprise.

But he couldn't, after all. The long tormenting day went by, with no chance to escape. His mother's friends met them from church. In the afternoon they drove to the sea, and it was supper-time when they got back. Would he have to wait till they were all *asleep*?

No: his luck changed. There was something they wanted to see on television. As they settled down, with their cups of tea, he held his breath. In a moment, Mum would look round and say, "Coming, Ran?" He must be gone before that.

Outside it was twilight already. Clouds had been rolling up all the afternoon. Now there were deep rumbles of thunder out at sea: a big storm was coming.

He had almost reached the garden door at Timewells when he started back, listening. Was that a footstep on the other side? Yes – the door was opening. He was behind the nearest tree in a second.

A small dark figure crept through, and stood by his tree, so close that he could hear it draw a long breath, nerving itself to move again. Then it darted across the lane and began to walk quickly away.

He had taken two steps in pursuit when something else happened: something so queer, so unexpected, that he could hardly believe what he saw.

Baggins had been over on the far side of the field. Now there came a thud of hooves, and he galloped out of the dusk, running by the fence, whinnying a greeting. Ran backed to the tree again. What in the world had got into Baggins? He only carried on like that over one person – and *she* was hundreds of miles away in France.

But the joyful huffling went on. Then he heard something else: the squeak of the latch on the field gate. He
looked round the tree. The hurrying child had turned
back, it was opening the gate, leading Baggins out, patting
him and talking to him. Then it was on his back. Pony and
rider moved out of sight down the lane.

Ran was gasping – No! No, it can't be! Not Arabella!

But he knew it was.

Only Arabella could have done all that so swiftly and
neatly; because she and Bags had set off together countless
times already.

But Arabella – here by herself, *by herself*? Hiding in her
own home? – when she was supposed to have been at
Sauterelle for two days? And where in the world was she
off to now?

His head seemed to spin. He set out to run after her –
then he had a better idea. He'd get his bike, and trail her
on that.

Whatever might be going on, he didn't mean to be left in
the dark any longer.

13

Night ride

Arabella couldn't wait for proper darkness. She must get the letter posted, and be home before the storm broke. That was going to be nasty enough, all alone in the house – out of doors it would be far worse.

She still felt a bit jumpy after the morning's adventure. It had ended all right: she'd stayed in hiding until Ran went away. But that seemed enough for one day, and now there would be thunder and lightning as well – really it didn't seem fair.

Outside it was still twilight; people would be about. She wouldn't risk the village post-box – she'd go the other way, through the lanes, to a little box she'd seen in a farmhouse wall.

The moment she stepped into the lane, Baggins heard her. She hadn't thought of that. He came galloping, whinnying at the top of his voice. She whispered crossly:

"Oh Bags, do shut up. You can't come – "

Then she thought – Yes, he can! Of course he can – and I'll put him in the stable, after, and stay there myself! So I shan't be alone in the storm – and nor will he, dear old fellow.

They set off at a steady trot, keeping on the grass at the roadside. There were headlights in the distance, on the main road, and she held her torch ready in case a car came.

They reached the post-box, and she leaned over to push

the letter in. She heard it flop down, and sighed with relief. At last it was on its way: the van would pick it up in the morning.

She patted Baggins, and he put his head down to snatch a mouthful of clover. The pony books said he mustn't do that; but he and she didn't always stick to the rules.

Suddenly she heard a little sound behind her. A faint grinding, like a foot touching the loose grit on the edge of the road. Looking back, she thought someone was there, on a bike. Waiting, with one foot on the ground . . .

Swiftly she made up her mind – she wouldn't go back that way. She'd go on to the cross-roads, and turn back up Copsewood Lane, and round by Squerries. She clutched the halter, whispered to Baggins and got his head up. Still munching, he moved off amiably. The cross-roads lay just ahead, round a corner.

She was almost there when she saw the gang.

A row of dark figures stood there, silent, leaning on the bank. No one moved as she came near. A long row of white faces turned to watch. It was eerie. She touched Baggins with her heel to make him hurry.

The line of faces puzzled him. He tossed his head, half-turned himself and went by in a shallow curve, like a banana, looking at them. Still no one spoke. Arabella thought – they seem to be waiting for something to happen.

And they were. They were waiting for last night's motor-bike gang: out for trouble, in fact. Their fathers, guessing as much, had locked up their motor-bikes. All the same, they'd gone out to wait.

Pony and rider were nearly past when one of the dark forms sprang to life. A voice called, "Hey. That's Buckleys' pony. Who's on him, then?"

Another voice drawled, "Young Ran of course. Who d'you think?"

Laughter. And then a mocking yell – "Thief! Stop thief!"

The rest took up the cry. All at once they were pelting after Baggins, whooping and screeching.

Baggins hadn't liked the look of them. Now he broke into a trot, then a canter, snorting in alarm. Arabella looked back, and saw that they were gaining . . . they were all so big, their legs so long. And one of them had a bike. It was coming faster and faster, ahead of the rest.

And Baggins was old. How long could he keep up this pace?

They swerved into Copsewood Lane. She had a moment's frantic hope – would the hunt go the other way? But no: they were coming on, baying like hounds, shouting "Yoicks" and other hunting noises.

The lane ran through a high copse. Now they were in a tunnel of darkness, Baggins still going his best. She crouched low, whispering, "Oh Bags, oh Bags, oh, oh, oh . . ." She felt stiff with terror, like a hunted fox. They musn't catch her: one glimpse of her face, and the secret would be done for.

Then a hand came out of the dark, and gripped the halter.

Baggins plunged and stopped. Arabella shrieked and kicked out wildly. Her foot struck metal. A bike. *That* bike! A voice hissed:

"I'll take him. Change over, see? – take the bike – hide – *get* on, quick!" And then – "It's me, Ran Atkins – "

"Ran!" she gasped.

There wasn't time for more. He pulled her off Baggins and jumped up in her place, and she heard him say, "Come on, boy." They were gone, in a skitter of dust: she was left clutching the bike. The whole thing had only taken a moment.

She backed into the darkness, under a tree, and stood there unseen as the hunt streamed past, with shouts and pounding feet – never dreaming that they'd changed foxes.

Ran! Ran Hat! It was so staggering, she couldn't take it in. He'd been following her – it was Ran she'd heard, then, when they stopped at the post-box. And he knew her all right. But how could he – when he thought they were all away?

And she'd always thought he hated all the Buckleys. All except Berry, anyway. And yet here he was, a friend, on her side, dashing to the rescue – knowing she musn't be caught. So he'd found out everything already ... ?

Then all at once the sky was filled with lightning. A long roll of thunder followed. She turned the bike, scrambled on and fled for home, shutting her eyes at each jagged flash, gritting her teeth and cowering from the crash of thunder.

She was just inside the garden when the rain began. Quick, the stable ... she got herself and the bike under cover and stood trembling. The rain came down like a waterfall; the gutters sang and gurgled, trees tossed and roared in the deluge, lightning danced and thunder echoed through the downs. And where, in all this uproar, were Ran and Baggins?

A lull: she took her hands away from her ears and listened. Yes – she could hear a faint clicking out in the lane. Baggins's footsteps: she knew those, just as he knew hers. The garden door swung open, and she ran out calling softly, "In here! In here!"

Poor, poor Bags, she thought – he must be nearly dead. She shone her torch on the pair as they stumbled into shelter.

What she saw was so surprising, she could only blink and stare.

Drowned rats, they looked like, yes; but as merry as grasshoppers and very pleased with themselves. Ran was *laughing*. So, in his own way, was Baggins. As she hugged him, he went *ho-ho-ho* and tossed his head, drenching her. Idiots! What was there to laugh at?

Ran gasped, "He went like a racer – they never caught up – then it came on to rain, they all cleared off – "

So they'd been enjoying themselves, while she was so scared and worried. And now Bags might be getting pneumonia or something worse, *glanders* or *staggers* . . . Too furious to speak to them, she stuck the torch into a crack, dragged out an armful of old sacks and went grimly to work on his coat.

Ran pulled off his soaking anorak and came to help. Well – of course, he'd been helping all along. Her spurt of temper died away as they mopped and scrubbed and brushed, first with sacks and then with twists of straw, and tied on more sacks for a rug. When Baggins nuzzled his water-bucket, she cried:

"Oh, but he ought to have something hot! Bran mash . . . come on, we'll boil the kettle – "

Ran pulled out his key. In the kitchen, while the kettle hummed, she ran her torch along the larder shelves, and pounced on a packet of oatmeal.

"Gruel – that's just as good as bran mash. Don't you think? Switch on the stove, Ran, I'll mix it up – "

"What's gruel?" he asked.

"It's – well, it's – sort of thin porridge. I think."

"Yuk. Sounds gruesome."

"You needn't have any." Then she laughed. "We'll have instant soup, French onion. Oh, and crisps, and cheese . . . I'm starving, are you?"

"Watch out," he warned. "You're doing it again."

"What? What am I doing?"

He was picking up oatmeal from the floor. He said, "It's a tip-off, d'you see? My mother's bound to notice, some time."

Arabella gaped at him. She stammered, "But – I haven't –

I never left a thing! I cleared it all up, every crumb, every scrap!"

"Except," he grinned, "the ones you missed."

"You mean – so *that* was it! That was how you knew – how you found out–"

Just as she said *found out*, they both started. Out in the passage, the phone began to ring.

They listened, quaking. The ringing went on and on, shrill and menacing. It seemed to say – *I know you're there. I'm waiting.*

Ran muttered, "It's all right. Wrong number – it'll stop in a minute–"

But it didn't stop. She whispered:

"Ran – your mother? *Could* she know you're here?"

"*No*. They're watching the box. Be there till midnight." Then he added slowly, "And – what about *your* mother? Does *she* know you're here?"

Arabella was dumb. The torch slipped through her fingers and cracked on the floor. The oatmeal plopped and seethed, the kettle clicked off. Still the ringing persisted.

Suddenly neither of them could bear it any longer. They seized the kettle, the pot and the rest, and tiptoed guiltily away into the swimming dark.

14

Haunted

Timewells felt like enemy territory now; but the stable was still a haven. They barred the door and switched on the light. If anyone came, Arabella could hide behind the hay-bales: but who would come, in this storm? The drumming rain, the sluicing trees, shut out all other sounds. The phone could ring for ever and they needn't know.

Baggins drank his gruel with pleased slurping noises. They relapsed into giggles, slurping their own soup. Perched on the hay, they picked up their talk where the ringing had disrupted it.

"Ran – I was so careful! So where did I slip up?"

"You did all right. Mum never noticed a thing. Only – " he explained about Bear, the missing postcard, the clues in the kitchen. "And then I saw your torch, last night, up in the attic. Of course I never thought it was *you* – we thought you were in France . . ."

"Yes, well. I'm supposed to be. You see – "

She went through it calmly, from the moment when Mum's letter had dropped on the mat in London.

It was easier than telling Ned or Karen. They'd have put on their silly-young-Arab airs. Ran was amazed, and impressed, seeing just how it all happened, taking it for granted he'd go on helping. In fact – she could see – he was really pleased to be in the secret.

(Ran Hat, of all people! They'd got him quite wrong, all this time.)

When she came to the secret key he exclaimed, "A key! Oh, then that's all right. I couldn't make out – "

"So when did you guess it was me? Oh – was it Baggins?"

"Who else? All that fuss and fuffle – I thought he was off his head. Till I saw he wasn't."

Baggins pricked his ears, kicked the empty pot away and strolled over, dribbling gruel, nuzzling for crisps.

"Rain's stopped," Ran said suddenly. He went to the door and listened. "Phone's stopped too."

Arabella didn't move. She said, "Think I'll stay here with Bags."

"All night? But you'll freeze!"

"I'd rather."

He was puzzled. "Bags'll be all right!"

"Oh, *he* will . . ." She hadn't meant to explain, but she heard herself whispering,

"I – can't go in there. Not in the dark. There's a ghost."

"In the *house*?" He was taking it seriously, with deep interest, as he'd taken everything else. "I never knew that – I thought it was just – you know – the garden . . ."

"On the landing," she persisted. "I saw it, last night. I opened the trap, and it was waiting – " She stopped in dismay. Ran was laughing outright.

"But that was *me*!"

"What?"

"Yes, I – I thought *you* were a ghost. The light in the attic, I mean. But I had to go up and see. And when you yelled – I saw it was . . . it was someone like us, so I waited till morning . . ." He found he couldn't say, *I panicked and ran home*.

Arabella leaned back with a sigh of relief. Timewells was safe again. She needn't give another thought to ghosts. At least – she sat up with a jump –

"Ran! What did you mean, just now – about the garden?"

He looked at her oddly: surprised, she could see. "But – haven't you ever – "

Suddenly enlightened, she broke in – "thought it was haunted? Yes, of course." Of course: she seemed, all at once, to have known that for years.

She said slowly, "When I'm out there – I keep thinking about the Shelleys . . . is it one of them?"

"I don't know. Who are the Shelleys?"

"You never heard of them?"

He shook his head. "No one called that, not round here."

"Well, you know that count-up they do – when you have to write down who's in your house, on a special night – ?"

"Oh, the census! There was one when I was – nine, I think – 1981? Mum had a form to fill up –"

"Yes, and 1881. And the Shelleys lived here then, in our house. Dad's got it all written down – their names and ages, and there were three girls – "

"But," Ran interrupted, "I thought it was all dead secret? Everything you put on that form?"

"It's secret for a hundred years, then anyone can look it up. So Dad looked up Timewells, and – " She had been fingering something in her pocket. Now she took it out. "Here – did you ever find any of *these*?"

He looked at the shell, and nodded. "They're all about, aren't they?"

They were silent. *All about* . . . the remark had a kind of echo.

"Oh . . . the Shelleys!" He saw what she was thinking. "D'you think *they* hid them, then? Because of the name – "

"As – sort of – tokens, yes. But – have you found any with a letter scratched on?"

He smiled. "A's, mostly. A few J's."

"Mm. But who was *A*, then? J could be Jane – but the other two were Eliza and Mary Ellen . . ."

"*I* thought the A's were yours . . ."

He said after a moment, "We could ask Mrs Bristowe."

"Who – ?"

"She keeps a lot of old stuff – scrapbooks, all about Timber. Old photos. Tapes of old people, nattering away . . . she might know something."

After a pause he asked, "Ever been up in Squerries?"

Again, he seemed to look at her oddly. She said in surprise:

"The beeches? Of course, why?"

"In summer, have you?"

"Why?" As he didn't answer, she tried to remember – "Winter, I think. We go up there for holly, there's always masses, no one else picks it – "

"No."

"*Oh*," she breathed, "you mean it's haunted too?"

"Only in summer. So they say. But people don't go there much, any time."

"But – you've been? You've seen it?"

"Not *seen* . . . d'you see anything, in the garden?"

"No. No. (Only those shells.) I just think about those girls – their games, you know. As if," she discovered, "as if they were *me*, in a way. But – as if they – *it* – would do the same things, even when I'm not there."

A swirl of raindrops raced across the roof. When the sound died away, Ran spoke. "It's summer now."

She picked up what he hadn't said. "If no one goes in Squerries – I could go. No one would see me . . . would you come?"

"Tomorrow," Ran said.

15

Annunziata

Tomorrow brought sunshine and clear skies. The beeches in Squerries glittered; mist floated up in wisps like smoke.

Not a morning to stay indoors. She was feeling restless – reckless, even. If only they could go up into Squerries *now*. But Ran couldn't get away. He was on nettle-slashing, he said: that meant clearing up the churchyard, with the Rector as gang-leader. Ned and Karen had helped in other years: *she* could have joined in, if only . . .

They'd agreed to meet this evening. She could slip out the back way, along the hedges, up to the edge of the wood. Gazing out of the west window, she plotted her course. Hours and hours to wait, though. She sighed impatiently.

Suddenly she stopped moping, and stared in disbelief. A child with a green face was running up the lane. It was gone before she could get a proper look, but another came after it. She wasn't dreaming: both had green goblin faces.

Then came a string of others – a space creature, a vampire, a dragon, a wolf. Of course: they were wearing masks off cornflake packets.

She sat on the floor and went on thoughtfully with her breakfast.

Masks, she thought. If I wore a mask, people wouldn't know me. I could go shopping, I could go anywhere, not just Squerries. The village might be a bit risky – but I could take Ned's bike. Fitching – that's not too far. Or Beaumarsh . . .

In books, girls cut their hair short and dressed as boys, and no one recognized them; but that was no good any more. Boys and girls dressed the same, and their hair was the same too: it was *faces* that gave you away. If I could cover up my face – ?

Not a cornflake mask: not at her age. But there were dressing-up things in the chest on the landing. Rummaging, she found a black velvet mask – Ned had been a highwayman at a Christmas party. No use, it would make people stare – just what she didn't want.

These might be better: large sun-glasses, a black curly wig. She put them on, and tucked her straight fair hair out of sight.

The effect was startling. She didn't look dark like Karen – she looked completely different. Staring at herself in Mum's long glass, she thought – I look like Annunziata! (the Italian *au pair* girl they'd had before Ginette). Or I would, if I could go brown . . .

Then she remembered – there's that cream Mum uses on the beach! Sun-Glow. She'd seen a tube of it in the bathroom cupboard. Yes, here it was: she squeezed, and the stuff came out like chocolate toothpaste.

The directions said: "Perfect tan. No sunburn. Smooth on evenly. Washes off easily."

Ten minutes later, the glass showed a dark-haired girl with brown face, hands and ankles. Arabella had disappeared. Vanishing-cream, she thought, and grinned in triumph.

She remembered just two words from Annunziata's stay: "*Meraviglioso*" and "*Guardi!*" If they meant "Smashing" and "Watch out" – then they said exactly what she felt.

She zipped her purse into her pocket and put on the sun-glasses.

79

Downstairs she found a postcard on the mat, addressed to herself, with "Please forward" under the address. The message was brief: "May we borrow Baggins again? Love, Sybil."

Sybil was the owner of the riding-school. Each year, in August, Baggins stayed there to teach the smallest riders about bending, musical posts and the other gymkhana games; he was clever at that. Of course he could go again! – she'd get Ran to ride him over. If only she could go too – but her disguise wasn't good enough for that.

She groaned, and dropped the card back on to the mat. She knew better, now, than to take it away: Mrs Hat would have heard the post van call here . . . And the grandfather clock had stopped, but she mustn't wind it.

The phone began to ring.

She gulped in alarm, and then stood shivering. It rang and rang, as it had done last night. Silly to take any notice – it couldn't be for her? – but again she felt threatened, hunted, terrified.

It stopped at last, and she escaped.

Ran had put Baggins back in the field; so she couldn't go out that way. He'd be sure to come galloping again – you couldn't fool *him* with a wig and a squeeze of Sun-Glow. She hauled out Ned's bike, mounted by the stable gate and went spinning away, along the church path, out to the top lane, down to Beaumarsh. *Free.* It felt glorious.

The little shop on the harbour wall was crammed with people in sailing gear, buying stores and bottles, and tourists buying postcards and telescopes. No one took any notice of her. She collected a loaf, eggs and butter, packets of nuts and raisins, a can of lemon drink. All that could go in the saddle-bag.

Waiting in the queue to pay, she read the posters on the walls: tide tables, a notice about the regatta, and another headed "Red Squirrel Watch". She read this one again.

It said that Sussex had once been "a haunt of red squirrels", but they'd all disappeared forty years ago. Now several pairs had been set free in local woods: naturalists were hoping they'd settle there and breed.

"If you see a red squirrel," it ended, "please write and tell us where, and what it was doing." There was an address to write to.

Speeding home, she thought – I'll do this every day. I'll ride to Westdean and Charlton, and watch for squirrels. No need to stay cooped up any more . . . the shopping trip had been a huge success.

She stopped to drink her lemonade, propped against a bridge over a stream. Presently there were voices behind her; in the handlebar mirror, she saw three more bikes approaching. Three girls ambled past. They smiled and said "Hullo!"

Arabella had a moment's doubt, in case they'd seen through the disguise: they were from the village, she knew *them* at once. Then she plucked up courage, and smiled back.

She recalled another of Annunziata's words, "*Ciao*," and said that, instead of "Hullo."

A mistake.

They turned back, propping themselves and their bikes on either side of her. Sweets were passed round. Friendly questions began.

"Italiano? Staying round here?" She nodded, then quickly shook her head.

They laughed. "Which?"

Watch out, she told herself, blushing in panic under the Sun-Glow.

"Down at Beaumarsh?"

This time it seemed safe to nod.

"We live at Timber. Know it?"

She tried a timid smile. They went on chatting. "That's a

smashing bike." "Did you sail over?" And then –

"I'm Liz, they're Kate and Alex. And you're –?"

"Annunziata," she said firmly.

Then something frightening happened. The girl named Kate, egged on by the others – "Let's hear you, then" – "Yes, come on" – "Your mum says you're *fluent*" – began, blushing in turn, to speak what could be nothing but Italian. Worse – she was obviously asking more questions, pausing for Arabella to reply.

There was a terrible silence: just as terrible for Kate: she was trying so hard, and "Annunziata" couldn't understand a word.

It was the real, long-ago Annunziata who came to the rescue. Before she knew what she was going to say, Arabella remembered the right words:

"Please. I must to speak English. I have promise."

If only she could copy Annunziata's voice, her dazzling smile . . . She did her best. Kate said with relief, "Oh, *scusi*. I had to promise too." Liz said, "Oh, come on, let's have a cooler. OK, Annunziata? A *paddle*," – with a schoolmistressy air – "in the *stream* . . ."

It was all right . . . she only had to join in their laughter. *Meraviglioso*.

All the same, they weren't getting her into the stream. She remembered the words on the Sun-Glow label: Washes off easily. Sun-glasses came off easily, too, when people started larking about in the water. And wigs? She hung back, fiddling with the straps of the saddle-bag.

As soon as the three were sitting on the bank, their feet in the stream, she jumped on and sped away as fast as possible.

No good. A moment later she heard them in pursuit – "Hi! Hey! Annunziata – wait!"

They caught her up, crying, "Look – you're going the wrong way for Beaumarsh – did you know? Shall we come back with you?" And, at last – "Where did you say you were staying?"

She tried a head-shake, another timid smile; but then they looked at her, worried: "Have you forgotten? Are you lost? Not to worry – "

If only they weren't so friendly!

Not far from Timber now. She'd have to turn and go all the way back to Beaumarsh – but suppose they insisted on coming too? She gasped, "Is quite all right. You are so kind. I – I just go for a ride – "

"Oh! That's OK then." But they were still with her. She turned towards Copsewood Lane; they turned too. Now there was a long hill . . .

The three began to race, speeding ahead, downhill. She went slowly, slowly, gripping the brakes. They were round a corner, out of sight for a moment. Then she saw the gate into Squerries Wood.

It stood a little way open. She threw herself off the bike, pushed it through the gap, squeezed after it, pulled the gate shut and flicked the wire loop over the post. The hedge was thick and high. She crouched behind it, listening.

"Annunzi-a-ta! Where – are – you?"

They were back, toiling up again, round the corner; calling to her and to each other. She heard the swish of tires coming near, going past, going away. Laughter and voices, further and further off.

They were *gone*.

16

Squerries

She hid there for a long time. It wouldn't do to risk meeting those three again. But how was she to get home?

A bird was calling from the high wood – "Here, here, here, here." Listening, she realized – I needn't go back yet. I can stay in the wood, and have a picnic. Or slip home through the fields. Or whatever I feel like. The sense of freedom came flooding back.

She set off up the steep path into the high beechwood. The bird seemed to follow overhead. A thrush, it must be – they often seemed to be singing real words, like this. A wild piping call – more like spring than late July.

And yet – could it be a bird? Sometimes the words were so clear: "Where – are – you?" – thin and far-away, like the three girls in the lane. And then, "I-can-see-you", over and over, like a child playing. She seemed to feel watching eyes; then she heard a soft chirrupping sound, like a monkey, or someone pretending to be a monkey.

As she peered upward, there was a tiny snapping noise, and a twig fell at her feet. Then something else: she felt a light sharp scratch on her hand, as it glanced off. A fir-cone.

A fir-cone? From a beech tree?

Then she shook herself, and laughed. There must be a squirrel up there. And the bird was a storm-cock, pleased about last night's rain.

Of course she couldn't help remembering what Ran had said. Was this really a haunted wood? Shadowy and mysterious, yes, like all woods in summer; and with secrets of its own, perhaps. But not frightening ones – she felt quite safe and happy.

And she was close to home. Timewells lay far below at the foot of the hill, almost like a doll's house. And there in the lane she saw three bikes go by, heading for the village. So she'd given them the slip. And the disguise had worked.

She pulled off glasses and wig, and looked about for somewhere to sit and get cool.

Just ahead lay a great beech tree, blown down in a gale, making a bridge across a ferny dell. A good place to hide the bike. She lowered it into the bracken, and started to cross the bridge.

Half-way over, there was a jagged hole where part of the tree had split away long ago, leaving a deep hollow. It was full of dry sticks and feathers. Jackdaws' nests.

She thought, in sudden excitement – jackdaws were like magpies, sometimes they stole bright objects and hid them in their nests. There might be a diamond ring, a gold brooch, a spade guinea . . . anything.

She picked out the sticks with great care, afraid she might find a rat or a snake as well; but she didn't. What she found seemed far more breathtaking than gold or diamonds.

As she cleared out the nests – countless years of nests, she thought – the hollow changed from a litter-bin to a deep dry cave; a secret den, big enough to hide in. Right at the end, she found the parcel.

At first it seemed just a bundle of old rubbish. She picked it up gingerly, to sling it out with the sticks; then she realized that there was something hard and square inside. She peeled away the wrappings – ancient newspapers, hardened into a kind of tree-bark, and rags of stuff that might have been skin or fur. Underneath was a rusty tin, like a tea canister, with a square lid that had once been sealed with some sort of plaster. This came away in fragments, but the lid was rusted on, she couldn't move it.

After breaking two finger-nails, she rushed back to the bike and rummaged in the saddle-bag, throwing the contents out, almost sobbing with impatience. String, band-aids, fruit-gums, a spanner, matches – yes! she found what she'd hoped for: Ned's old penknife.

It took a long struggle – jabbing, prising, scraping, straining – to get the lid off. Inside was another, smaller package. Another box? Trembling, she unfolded more wrappings; skin and fur, again, still intact, because they'd been sealed so carefully in the canister.

At last she could see what lay inside. A book. Only an old book. Nothing else. Shabby and faded, with a title she couldn't read.

She felt a pang of disappointment. But then she picked it up and opened it. Something flashed up at her from the title page, and she gasped out loud. Her own name. There it was in print: *"Life And Her Children.* By Arabella Buckley."

It couldn't be true – how could it? She turned the pages at random. Some of them were stuck together; but she could make out enough to see that it was a book about nature. Sea life, chiefly, sponges and shells.

Shells . . . with a flash of hope, she turned back to the fly-leaf. But it was more than hope: before she read the name there, she knew what it would be. Shelley.

The inscription was still clear as the day it had been written, in pen and ink – brown and faded, like the book itself, but perfectly readable: "Ary Shelley, from her friend Mark Erskine. 10th April 1882."

Ary. *A for Ary.* A book about shells. By Arabella Buckley.

She sat for a long time without moving, just holding the book and trembling with excitement, turning a page sometimes, looking at drawings of sea urchins and jelly-fish and an octopus. Slowly, there came an indistinct memory – Mum telling her that Grandma, or Great-Grandma, had had a history book by someone called Arabella Buckley, and they'd thought it was a good name for *her*; so that was how she came to be another Arabella. All the same, it was eerie – to come on your own name, printed in an old, old book.

And it had belonged to Ary Shelley. "From her friend Mark Erskine." Who were *they*? Ary must have climbed this tree, and left her book here, in its wrappings . . . why?

Had she lived at Timewells like the others – she must be a relation? And what had become of her; and who was Mark Erskine? Something so carefully packed up, so cleverly hidden, must have been precious to the owner – so why hadn't she kept it . . . ?

The questions came crowding into her mind, and there were no answers: perhaps there never would be. But what a find, to show Ran!

This den, too – what a find that was; almost as thrilling as discovering Ary's name, and Ary's cache. She'd always wanted a pad of her own, outdoors somewhere, that the others didn't know about. She laid the book down care-fully, and looked about for ways to make it better still.

Far down the slope there was a clearing where the sun had dried the undergrowth. She pulled armfuls of bracken for a carpet, and sheets of moss to line the craggy walls, and pink rosebay petals to make patterns on the moss, like wallpaper.

One wall had an ornament already: a huge beetle – a stag-beetle? – with the right kind of antlers for a doll's country house. Was it alive? She breathed on it, and the antlers waved drowsily. Then it was still. It hung there, glossy and elegant, like a chocolate frog out of a Christmas stocking.

The thought of chocolate suddenly made her hungry. She picked some wild raspberries, and rescued the bag of eatables, thrown out of the saddle-bag while she was rummaging. Then she noticed the box of matches.

Matches! She could light a fire and make toast.

The tree, as it fell, had scooped out a ball of earth, leaving a deep crater: a safe fire-place, ready made.

The jackdaw twigs were just right for kindling, with dry fern, then thicker sticks and bits of bark. Soon a good fire was blazing. If anyone saw the smoke, they'd only think it was mist.

She put eggs to roast, and peeled a stick for a toasting-fork.

The first egg was a disaster. It cracked, hissed and burst, dissolving into black powder. She pricked the next two with a sharp thorn, then wrapped them in moss and mullein leaves, as carefully as Ary Shelley had wrapped her book. Now they baked away quietly in the ashes and came out red-hot on the outside, succulent inside. Curled on the bracken couch, she ate them with toast and butter and raspberries.

Bluetits came flitting about, and she ran across the bridge to scatter nuts and raisins for them at the far end. Then she had her third find.

It was in a little niche, where the trunk tapered away under the topmost branches, forming a cup that brimmed with rain. Something was floating on the dark water. She scooped it out.

A shell. A tiny shell, so frail and old that it seemed ready to melt away at her touch. She looked inside, and saw a faint mark there, the mark she expected to see: an A.

She carried it back, and laid it in a cranny beside the stag-beetle.

What a climber Ary must have been! – to get so high up, and leave her token there in triumph. Looking round at the other trees, Arabella wondered how many of them, in their topmost nooks and crannies, still kept a hidden shell. Again, she might never know – she didn't think she would dare to go so high. Perhaps Ran – ?

She found herself dozing, dreaming, half-aware of other creatures around her. A wood-pigeon, on a distant bough, turned this way and that to catch the sun, like a lady on the beach at Sauterelle. Rabbits skipped in the clearing. Once she heard footsteps, and shrank back into the cave; but it was only a little roe deer, stepping daintily, browsing on the raspberry bushes.

Now she was dreaming about voices in the trees, chanting, and chattering softly. She woke with a start: but it wasn't all a dream. The soft chattering sound had been real, she could still hear it, coming from a tall beech down at the edge of the clearing.

Then she sat up. Something was running on the tree. A weasel – she'd seen one in a tree before, and it was this colour, russet-brown, and creamy underneath. But – she'd never seen a weasel with a tail like that! Large and fluffy and wavy, more like a squirrel's. If it had been grey, she'd have known it *was* a squirrel, but –

Then she understood.

She remembered the poster in the shop at Beaumarsh: "Red Squirrel Watch". For the first time in her life, she was seeing a red squirrel. Two red squirrels . . . no, three, four, five of them: they followed each other down the tree and came springing and scampering towards her.

Holding her breath, she watched them jump on to the bridge . . . the chattering sound came from the first, the leader, and it was bigger than the rest. It must be their mother.

A whole family of red squirrels. It was like a miracle. One of those new pairs had found its way here, to Squerries, and made a home, and raised a family. And they'd stay on, she felt sure. Here there was everything they could want, beech-nuts, hazel-nuts, fir-cones, berries of all kinds. And peace. Ran said hardly anyone came here, because it was supposed to be haunted.

Well – and so it was, now. For the first time for forty years, Squerries was "a haunt of red squirrels". *Squerries* – could that be a country name for squirrels? Had they lived here in Ary's time – had she come here to watch them, too...?

Arabella sat in a dream. They were all on the bridge now; they danced along and found the nuts and raisins, and began to eat. First one, then another, they picked up the nuts in their paws and sat up to nibble, like Squirrel Nutkin with the robin's-pincushion.

They ran about, licking up egg crumbs, flirting their beautiful tails, pricking their soft tufted ears, frisking and cavorting, gazing about from brilliant dark eyes.

The mother ran further along the tree-trunk, calling to the young ones to follow. She came so near that Arabella could see the single hairs on her glossy coat. The fur was almost orange colour – like a fox or a marmalade cat – and her long nails were curved like young rose-thorns, gripping and skittering on the bark.

She didn't see Arabella. She skipped round the front of the cave, and out of sight. The four little squirrels came jumping after her. Then they were all gone. Arabella could hear the sound of claws overhead, like birds walking on a roof, and that soft scolding chatter ... then silence.

Still she sat there, not daring to move in case they might be near. She gave a long, long sigh; she seemed to be aching, not just from keeping still, but from sheer happiness.

At last she crept out. They were nowhere to be seen; she strained her ears, and couldn't hear the chattering any longer. All around, the dark summer leaves hung and whispered.

They hadn't really gone: they were living here, and she'd see them again. This evening, perhaps, with Ran. And she'd tell the Red Squirrel Watchers – she'd write to them as soon as she got home.

Quickly she packed up the saddle-bag; the book went on top, its wrappings made secure with string. She felt that she'd never part with *that*, she'd keep it always, a memento of Ary and this happy afternoon.

She was ready to go, when a glimpse of herself in the handle-bar mirror made her stop short. Her disguise . . . she'd forgotten all about it. Her own hair fell about her ears; the Sun-Glow had all worn off. Anyone seeing her would say – "Why, Arabella Buckley!" And they wouldn't be talking about the author of *Life And Her Children*, or Great-Grandma's *History of England*.

But the sun-tan tube was in her pocket; soon her face again became Annunziata's. Now the wig, the sun-glasses: her mask was back in place.

As she made this transformation, the strange bird had begun to call again, somewhere overhead. It followed her down to the edge of the wood, as though it were saying, "Stay here, stay here. Don't go yet."

17

Ary

She reached Timewells by the back way, slipping behind hedges and along a cart track, into the church path. By the stable gate she hesitated. The nettle-slashers must have finished. They were gathered in front of the lych-gate, while Mr Fielding, the Rector, collected tools and stowed them in his van.

Could she signal to Ran, somehow? He must be there with the rest.

She scanned the crowd of teenagers from the village, and visiting boys, staying at the Rectory. No sign of Ran. A Chinese-looking boy ran out, waving a pair of shears, snapping them at the others. Mr Fielding grabbed them, telling him off in some foreign language – Chinese? – and herded the whole gang into the van. They'd be driving off to the Rectory for the tea that always followed nettle-slashing. But where was Ran?

Then she saw him, standing by the corner of the church, holding a billhook and looking wary. As soon as the van moved, he came pelting across and hopped over the wall. He was coming to Timewells.

Next moment he saw her standing in the pathway, and pulled up short. She said politely:

"*Scusi*, Signor. I am looking for a place called Timewells, do you know it?"

Ran said, "I know it, but – " He came nearer, he looked

Ned's bike over, and then herself. A grin slowly replaced his doubtful expression.

"Not bad . . . not bad at all! Where've you been – ?" Then he raced on, "I've found out something!"

"And *I*'ve found out something!"

They finished together with a rush – "*Ary Shelley*."

Arabella's face fell. "Where did *you* – ? I've found it in a book, come in, I'll show you – "

"No, wait. Come and see *this* first!"

He led her across the churchyard: close-shaven now, smelling of cut nettles and hogweed sap.

What he had found was a gravestone on a short green mound. The stone was covered with yellow lichen; the lettering had been scraped clean. She read:

ARY SHELLEY

1873–1884

As she didn't speak, he said at length – "You see? It's *her*, isn't it? That did those A's. Or *him*, I suppose it could be – "

"No. No, it's *her* . . ." She stared at the grassy mound. It was a shock, somehow, to realize that Ary must be dead. Up in the wood, with the cache and the shell, she'd seemed so real and alive.

"How do you know? Could be either. Ary . . . it's a queer name, isn't it?"

"It *is* a girl. I told you – it's in a book . . . but she's not one of ours. So why was she in our garden?"

"Cousin, perhaps? Played with them?"

"Yeees . . . can't we find out who her people were? What about – you know – those books they keep in the vestry? Like that register? That people have to sign at weddings – ?"

"She wasn't old enough – oh, I see . . ."

"Not for a wedding. But her funeral . . . would there be a register for *those*?"

"Vestry's locked," Ran said. "But – Mr Fielding – I'll ask

him. Get your bike, you can come too – "

"He might know me – ?"

"In that get-up? Has anyone else?"

"Not exactly . . . but . . ."

"Come on," he urged; and she came, too eager to be cautious.

The Rectory door stood open. A roar of voices, a clatter of plates and knives sounded from the kitchen at the back. Mr Fielding appeared with a teacup in one hand and a sandwich in the other, like the Mad Hatter.

"Well done – the missing weapon – " – he collected the billhook, and waved them in, smiling at Arabella: "Another visitor?"

Ran, unprepared, stood speechless. So, for a moment, did Arabella. She remembered the boy with the shears. If the Rector knew *Chinese*, Italian would be nothing – and he'd be sure to know a lot more of it than Kate. She let Annunziata go, and said "Anna" – and saw Ran's eyes widen. She'd scored again, for presence of mind this time.

Ran found his voice and plunged into explanations:

"Please, could you tell us – you see, there's this grave I saw. It says she died when she was – eleven – 1884. And we wondered – could we go in the vestry and look her up? – and find out who she was? – her father and mother, I mean . . ."

Mr Fielding took this calmly, as though requests like theirs happened all the time; as indeed they did. He said patiently:

"You can see the burial entry, certainly. In here – " He drew them into a room that might once have been the family dining-room; set his teacup on the window-sill, got rid of the sandwich in two bites, scoured his finger-tips with a handkerchief and turned to a glass-fronted cupboard. They saw rows of stiff-covered volumes, like ledgers. He found one with the label: *Burials. 1850–1899*, took it out and set it on the dining-table.

"The old books were getting frail, you see, so we've had them copied. Now, which year – 1884? What name?"

When they said, "Ary Shelley," he looked up. His face changed. He seemed suddenly excited.

"But – that's amazing! You've found her grave? Well, I can show you . . . but wait, have a look at this entry first. July 26th – I looked it up, only the other day – I'll tell you why in a minute. Here it is."

And there it was, in black type, on a page headed 1884.

Mary Ellen Shelley. Timewells. July 26. Age: 11.

Arabella cried out, "Mary Ellen! The youngest – it's her after all! And they lived at – at – " Just in time, she stopped herself: *our house* – she'd so nearly said it.

Ran came swiftly to her rescue. "Yes, Timewells. But – Mary Ellen – Ary – are they the same, then? It says Ary on the grave – ?"

"They *are* the same," Mr Fielding said. "And I'll show you how I know . . ." He had taken a folder from another cupboard. He brought it to the table, undoing the strings, talking all the while, as interested as they were themselves.

"I was looking through these, just the other day, I'm lending them to Denzil Riggs – he's doing research for a book – they're just a few relics that one of our Rectors left. Diaries, mostly – parish affairs. And I came across *this* . . . his sketchbook, when he was a curate."

He turned the pages. They saw black and white sketches, cottages, the water-mill, the church; and faded water-colour paintings, wild flowers, moths, shells . . . Arabella caught her breath. Looking closer, snatching off the dark glasses, she made out a name at the corner of a page. *Mark Erskine.* Ary's friend.

Mr Fielding came to the last painting. After that, the pages were blank.

It showed a beechwood in autumn. In the foreground a little girl sat on a log, feeding a tame red squirrel. She was barefoot, in a short russet-coloured dress, tangled hair falling on her shoulders. The same name appeared at one corner. Arabella couldn't speak, but she touched it with her finger-tip.

"Yes. Mark Erskine," Mr Fielding said. "He was curate here in the 80s. Rector afterwards, for a very long time . . . do you see who she is?"

They had seen at once. Under the picture was written: Mary Ellen Shelley. "Ary." October 1883.

There was something else, at the bottom of the page, in faded ink. Mr Fielding read it aloud.

23rd July 1884.   Then to the elements
                  Be free, and fare thou well.

He added slowly, "That must have been the date she died. A kind of epitaph. Prospero, saying goodbye to Ariel."

Ran asked uncertainly, "Is that – out of the Bible?"

"Shakespeare. *The Tempest.*" Mr Fielding glanced at Arabella's stricken face, and said gently, "Look here. I found this too."

It was an old diary, one of a bundle packed into the folder. On the shabby leather cover was the year in gilt: 1924. The page for July 23rd was covered in neat writing, the same as the writing under the picture, describing a village school outing. But again, in tiny letters at the foot of the page, there was another line:

40 years. Ary. Whom I have loved long since and lost awhile.

"Another epitaph . . . he was fond of the child, you see."

Arabella whispered, "He was her friend."

"Yes, so it seems . . ." Mr Fielding was packing up the

folder again. "But he never had a child of his own. Never married. No one ever claimed his things, when he died – they've been here ever since."

"But – " Ran looked at Arabella, and saw the same question in her face – "She was only eleven. What did she die of?"

The Rector shook his head. "Children did die, rather often, in those days. From quite ordinary things, sometimes – measles, and so on."

"And – can't we find out about that, too?" Ran persisted.

"Well, we can send for the death certificate. But that takes time. I wonder . . . Denzil Riggs, perhaps – "

Ran picked up the folder. "You said – you meant this for Mr Riggs? I'll take it over, shall I – *he* might know something?"

"He might indeed. Well, thanks, Ran – " He produced a roomy carrier bag and slipped the folder into it. "But – you won't be long? We start in about an hour, you know – and how about your tea?"

"Start for where?" Arabella asked, as they cycled up the lane.

"Oh . . . he's taking us to a disco – *them*, I mean . . . look," Ran said eagerly, "Let's try Mrs B. first, shall we?"

"Mrs B – ?"

"Bristowe. That keeps all those scrapbooks, for the Women's Institute. Village history . . . 's not far, we'll be there in no time – " Swinging the carrier, he turned down the valley road, and Arabella followed.

Absorbed in thoughts of Ary, she'd forgotten to worry about being recognized. Mr Fielding clearly hadn't known her – the disguise was still going well.

But Mrs Bristowe was another matter. She came as a shock to Arabella.

She lived in a flat in a country house, a mile from the village. As they raced up the drive, parked their bikes and

97

climbed a flight of steps to her door, Arabella had no misgivings. Without thinking, she pulled off the dark glasses again. The door opened at Ran's knock, and Mrs Bristowe stood there.

Arabella knew her at once. The lady in the train – that she'd escaped from, at Arundel. Her heart sank. She began to back away . . . but that would make things worse?

As Ran started to explain their errand, the keen blue eyes were scanning *her*: taking in, with bright amused glances, the wig, the make-up, her panicky expression. Their eyes met, and Arabella's grew wide with alarm.

If Ran hadn't spoken up so quickly, all might have been lost. But when she heard the words "village history" Mrs Bristowe seemed to prick her ears, like a dog that hears the lid being taken off a biscuit tin. The quizzing look wavered, and darted away.

Talking happily, she led them into a room like the one at the Rectory, lined with cupboards.

"Here we are – I'm archivist, you see, for our W.I. – we started right back in the 50s. Now! – is it for a holiday task – or don't you have those nowadays?"

But when Ran said "1884" she looked disappointed.

"*Not* a lot, I'm afraid . . . oh, but wait! The school – we've a photo, early 80s, I'm sure – "

"The school! Oh *yes*," Ran said. "She must have gone to school – "

They were gazing, a moment later, at an old photograph in an album. A caption said: *Timber and Milfold Church of England School, July 1883.* There, in faded sepia, stood rows of girls in long dark dresses and white pinafores, hair strained back from anxious faces; solemn little boys in thick jackets; all wearing heavy-looking boots.

Could Ary possibly be one of them? The group had been taken in the same year as Mark Erskine had painted her in a wood – in Squerries? – barefoot, carefree, feeding a squirrel, looking like a small gypsy. There seemed no gleam of likeness between *that* girl and any of these.

As they studied the picture, Arabella felt Mrs Bristowe's interest stray back to *her*. She looked up, and again she met that bright inquisitive gaze. The question – "Lucy Buckley's daughter?" – seemed to hover in the air. She trod on Ran's toe, caught his eye and signalled a frantic message – *Get us out of here*.

He turned to Mrs Bristowe. "I've just thought – when somebody dies – sometimes they write about them in the local paper. If we went to the newspaper office – d'you think they'd let us look at the old copies? You see, we want to know what she died of – "

"Local papers – of course!" Mrs Bristowe's attention was diverted once more. "But you needn't go to the office – I know the very person to help you, here in Timber. Denzil Riggs – "

"Oh, that's where we're going! Mr Fielding told us – "

"Yes, he's writing a book, you know, about our part of Sussex – and he's got *all* the local papers, a hundred years of them. I'm sure he'll help you . . . such a charming man . . ."

This was how they came to read the *Sussex Courier* for Tuesday, 29th July 1884.

Denzil Riggs lived in one of the old cottages by the mill, with purple clematis around the door and pink geraniums in the window. But, charming or not, there was nothing old-world about this alert, wiry-looking man; still less about his working methods.

They had supposed he would set them to search through dusty files or stacks of ancient newspapers. But they found themselves in what looked like a roomful of computers.

When he heard what they were looking for, Denzil Riggs tapped at a keyboard, read some numbers off the screen and produced a spool of film the size of a reel of sticky tape. He switched on another machine, slotted in the film, pressed another switch. A screen lit up; they saw a whole page of the *Sussex Courier* in miniature: column after column of tiny print.

Another flick, and the left-hand column swam up, large and clear, with the heading: Local Intelligence. It moved slowly upward as they watched. Names of towns and villages glided past. Breathless, they scanned headline after headline: Trespassing; Cricket; Stealing Firewood; Sheep Killed By Lightning; Cricket; Cottagers' Flower Show; Mr W. S. Blunt's Pure Arabs; Princess of Wales To Attend Races; Choir Outing; Cricket; Runaway Horse; Strange Assault On Schoolmaster . . .

Suddenly, at the foot of the third column, the movement halted. Print dazzled their eyes. Denzil Riggs said quietly:

"I think this is what we're after."

SAD FATALITY AT TIMBER. An 11-year-old girl, missing from her home on Wednesday evening, was found dead by her father under a tree in Squerries Wood. A jury sitting at the Fox Inn on Friday found that Mary Ellen Shelley, known to her friends as "Ary", died accidentally through falling from a tree. Medical evidence showed that death would have been instantaneous. The unfortunate father, Edward Shelley, said that as a child she had been in the habit of climbing in the wood, but he had supposed this pastime long outgrown. The girl was to have left home this week for a post in domestic service.

18

From sea to sea

Arabella let herself into the cottage and sat down at the foot of the stairs. She was very glad to be home: she seemed to have been away for a hundred years.

A hundred years . . . it was only then that she realized: this was the 23rd of July, 1984. On this day, in 1884, Ary had fallen out of a tree – that tree? – and died. But first, on the same day perhaps, she'd hidden her book, her present from Mark Erskine.

And *she* had found it, today.

For something to come to light, a hundred years on, seemed right and fitting, as though it had been meant to happen. Like a time capsule; like a spell in a fairy tale.

A faint sense of comfort stole through her at the thought. The shock of Ary's death – of reading about it, in print, on a video screen – began to fade. She found herself thinking – death is the wrong word, really. She's still here. Someone is, anyway. And *I* am. And so is Timewells. And the red squirrels are back, and I've found my den, I can go there and watch them. And it's all a secret; except for Ran, of course.

They'd go up there soon, as soon as he got here: he'd gone to tell Mr Fielding about the *Sussex Courier*. She pictured Ran's surprise. And he hadn't seen Ary's book yet. She was holding it now as she sat there. She'd find a new tin box for it, and put it back in their den in Squerries, so that it could belong to both of them. All of them.

The grandfather clock chimed softly. Mrs Hat must have wound it: Ran had said she'd been in here this afternoon. And she'd picked up Sybil's postcard from the mat – it would be on the telephone shelf.

Funny: it wasn't there. But that was her place for post-cards. What could she have done with it?

Then, with a pang of horror, she knew.

Sybil had written "Please forward" on the card – *and that was what Mrs Hat had done*.

She'd have written on a blank space, as usual – "All well here. H. Atkins." And put on another stamp, and dropped it in the box for the afternoon collection. It had gone off already – addressed to Sauterelle. Addressed to *her*.

But . . . at Sauterelle, they all thought Mrs Hat was looking after her: sleeping here, anyway, and getting meals. They thought that was what Dad and Mum had arranged. So – Mrs Hat would never have forwarded a card addressed "Arabella Buckley, Timewells."

And now, when it got there, the worst would happen. Ginette would be here to fetch her on the next plane. She'd known all along that that might happen, of course – but now, today, it was far worse than before. Now everything was perfect. She'd made friends with Ran, she'd invented a disguise, and she could go about with him – to Squerries, anyway.

And the squirrels . . . she couldn't bear to leave them, to lose it all, and go *there*. She told herself – I won't do it.

She felt tears coming, and dashed them away with her knuckles. No use *crying*. The thing was to make a plan. She'd escape, before Ginette got here, and live in her den . . . Ran would help . . .

There was a footstep outside: he was here already. The key scritched in the lock. As the door opened, she sprang up, calling:

"Oh Ran, listen. Something awful's happened . . ."

Then she stopped, gasped, and stared in astonishment.

It wasn't Ran in the doorway. It was Ned.

She cried out in despair –

"But it can't have got there yet!"

Ned blinked, and shook his head. His face looked pale, his eyes bloodshot, as though he were very tired. He stared back at her for a moment, without a word or a smile.

He must be pretty fed up with her. Well, of course he was – he'd had to come all this way to fetch her. (But how *had* they found out, then?)

He was carrying his large rucksack. Slowly he put it down; and then he seemed to flop down on to the door-mat, leaning back and shutting his eyes.

Somehow . . . he was different. More grown-up. But that was silly. He'd only been gone four days.

She nerved herself to say:

"I'm *not* going there. I won't. Whatever you say." But she saw it was no use. At last she couldn't bear the silence. She whispered miserably:

"When do we have to go?"

Again he shook his head; as though she wasn't talking sense.

"Go? Go where?"

"There, of course. Sauterelle." *He* wasn't making sense at all. He muttered something she couldn't catch.

"What?"

Eyes still shut, he said wearily:

"I said – I'm not going back."

So it was serious. "Ginette – Madame – are they furious with me, then?"

Suddenly he grinned. "Ginette will be. I expect. If she ever hears about those letters." He added with that grown-up air, amused and tired, and somehow out of reach –

"You've got a nerve, young Arabella."

"I haven't! I didn't – it was all an accident – "

"Typing those letters was an *accident*?"

"Not that, no. Of course not. But – how did you find out I'd done them?"

"Oh . . ." He shrugged. "Easy, when I looked at them. You did them on the old Remington. Wrong type, for Mum's little Adler."

"I know. I never meant – you see, it was just a sort of game. And then Berry went and found them – "

"Oh well." He yawned. "Lucky for me, as it's turned out. A good excuse to get away."

Get away? She stammered, "But, Ned – " and stopped. What was that he'd said – about not going back? It couldn't be true.

"Ned! What's happened?"

He stood up, saying listlessly, "Promised I'd ring Madame." He went to the telephone. And then she remembered that long, long ringing.

"Ned – was that you, trying to ring *me*? Last night – and this morning?"

"So you *were* here. Why not answer, then?"

"But I couldn't. I had to hide – "

"Ah yes. Oh well." He lifted the phone and began to dial, then to talk in careful French. Arabella could follow most of it. He was asking for Madame Rosier. A pause. Then –

"Ned here, Madame. I am now at home. Arabella is here, yes . . . I think not, Madame, thank you. Madame, I want to thank you again . . . And Monsieur too. Tomorrow I will write to my parents . . ."

At last he put down the phone. He said, quietly, "So that's that."

"But – you mean – you don't mean – *we can stay here*?" She was afraid to believe it, afraid to hope: afraid of something she didn't understand. Something wrong . . .

She whispered, "Ned? What did happen? Why aren't you going back?"

He only yawned again, and stretched. Then he said slowly:

"Oh . . . it was just boring. No fun at all. So I did a check in the travel file – just to see if my ticket would be OK, if I wanted to come home. And I found those letters of yours. So then of course I *had* to come, to see what you were up to."

"You told Ginette – ?"

"She was out. She and K. and Berry. Beach picnic. No fond farewells."

"You mean – you *ran away*?"

He said with dignity, "Of course not. I fixed it up with Madame. Told her there'd been a muddle, and you were here alone."

"Oh . . . I wasn't alone really. Ran Hat was all about."

"Ran Hat? What's he got to do with it?"

"Tell you after. Go on . . . was Madame ratty?"

"Not a bit. Not even *blessée*." He half-smiled, and began to talk more easily. "It did seem a bit off, two of us dropping out. Even if she can fill the place twice over. But she – " He stopped, and went on – "She was really nice. She said – she said – to come back another time . . . Well, and then Monsieur drove me to the airport, and I waited years for a seat, all night and then all morning – and . . ." Another great yawn. There were tears in his eyes. He finished curtly:

"I'm off to bed. See you tomorrow."

He was on the attic steps before she found courage to call –

"Ned. I've been in your room."

No answer. She heard the trap-door shut.

Ran didn't come, after all. He'd been roped in for that

disco trip. Or – perhaps, like herself, he'd suddenly felt tired out . . . with all that had happened.

As for Ned – no wonder he was tired, sitting up all last night.

Too tired to sleep well, it seemed. She woke more than once, and heard him moving about up there.

Then it was morning. Ned was calling down to her – "There's some junk of yours here. You can come and get it."

The attic looked different. At once she saw why: the portrait of Chantal was gone. Ned was at the table, working at a new poster, white lettering on black paper. It was a poem: *The Wandering Knight's Song*. The ink was still wet on the last verse:

I ride from land to land,

I sail from sea to sea ;

Some day more kind I fate may find

Suddenly she heard herself asking –

"Was it – did she – did you come away because of *her*? Chantal?"

Ned was standing with his back to her, staring out of the west window. There was a long pause. She thought he wasn't going to answer.

Then he said slowly, as though he could still hardly believe it –

"She sent me a message. By one of her gang. She said . . . not to follow her about, this time. Because I was . . . I was *too young* for them."

She found nothing at all to say. It seemed too terrible.

Looking again at the poem, she ventured at last:

"Aren't you going to finish it?" (There has to be another line. A happy ending, she thought.)

But Ned had dropped the brush. He said rather grimly:

"I think it will do as it is. For now."

*

It wasn't until later, down in the kitchen, over the tea mugs and egg-shells, that Arabella really took in how everything had changed.

Over breakfast, they'd written the letter to Dad and Mum, to say that they were both at home, and Madame understood, and they'd explain the whole thing when they were all together again. When this was sealed and stamped, Arabella said anxiously:

"Hadn't we better clear up soon? Mrs Hat will be in."

"Oh, leave it." (Ned sounded more like himself now. Not carefree – not yet; but as though he might be again, one day.) "Let's sling it all in the sink. Pity to waste the morning."

And then it dawned on her.

She needn't hide any more. She could go anywhere – to the village, the riding-school, Squerries – as *herself*. No need to dodge Liz and the other girls – or be scared of prying eyes like Mrs Bristowe's.

She laughed, "Oh Ned. Isn't it great –" and then stopped, feeling clumsy. What would *he* find to do? She asked carefully:

"Will you go wind-surfing?"

"Some time. Going to Beaumarsh now. Some chaps in my form have a boat there."

So that was all right.

Then he added with a sigh:

"I suppose you can come. If you must."

Arabella lifted her chin. "Afraid I'll be too busy."

"Ah. Doing what?"

"Taking Bags over to Sybil. They want him to stay again. We've a lot to do."

She hesitated. Should she tell him about the Red Squirrel Watch? No . . . she and Ran would keep that to themselves. She added:

"I'll be out all day, I expect."

107

"And how will you get back from Sybil's? Or will you doss down in the hay?"

She said in Ginette's voice, "No *problème*." And then – "I can hitch a lift from Ran Hat."

"Ran Hat – that sulk! Well well. So we're pals now, are we?"

"He's not a sulk. Not a bit, when you know him . . ." She giggled. "He thought I was a ghost. And I thought *he* was . . ."

"Oh yes? Go on."

"Oh . . ." She thought of the long four days. "No time now. I'll tell you when the others come home . . ."

Running up to find her riding-cap, she added quietly – "Some of it."

When the clap of the garden door died away behind them, Timewells sank back into its summer dream.

The greenfinches were trilling like canaries. Ripe seed-pods split and crackled like toy pistols. Something light as air was straying about the garden, picking loose honey-suckles, startling grasshoppers, breathing on moth and bumble-bee, stroking their fur the wrong way.

The trees stood about like tall sundials, marking out time with their shadows.